The Lazy Tour of Two Idle Apprentices

Charles Dickens

Copyright Notice

CONTENTS

CHAPTER I

In the autumn month of September, eighteen hundred and fifty-seven, wherein these presents bear date, two idle apprentices, exhausted by the long, hot summer, and the long, hot work it had brought with it, ran away from their employer. They were bound to a highly meritorious lady (named Literature), of fair credit and repute, though, it must be acknowledged, not quite so highly esteemed in the City as she might be. This is the more remarkable, as there is nothing against the respectable lady in that quarter, but quite the contrary; her family having rendered eminent service to many famous citizens of London. It may be sufficient to name Sir William Walworth, Lord Mayor under King Richard II., at the time of Wat Tyler's insurrection, and Sir Richard Whittington: which latter distinguished man and magistrate was doubtless indebted to the lady's family for the gift of his celebrated cat. There is also strong reason to suppose that they rang the Highgate bells for him with their own hands.

The misguided young men who thus shirked their duty to the mistress from whom they had received many favours, were actuated by the low idea of making a perfectly idle trip, in any direction. They had no intention of going anywhere in particular; they wanted to see nothing, they wanted to know nothing, they wanted to learn nothing, they wanted to do nothing. They wanted only to be idle. They took to themselves (after HOGARTH), the names of Mr. Thomas Idle and Mr. Francis Goodchild; but there was not a moral pin to choose between them, and they were both idle in the last degree.

Between Francis and Thomas, however, there was this difference of character: Goodchild was laboriously idle, and would take upon himself any amount of pains and labour to assure himself that he was idle; in short, had no better idea of idleness than that it was useless industry. Thomas Idle, on the other hand, was an idler of the unmixed Irish or Neapolitan type; a passive idler, a born-and-bred idler, a consistent idler, who practised what he would have preached if he had not been too idle to preach; a one entire and perfect chrysolite of idleness.

The two idle apprentices found themselves, within a few hours of their escape, walking down into the North of England, that is to say, Thomas was lying in a meadow, looking at the railway trains as they passed over a distant viaduct – which was HIS idea of walking down into the North; while Francis was walking a mile due South against time – which was HIS idea of walking down into the North. In the meantime the day waned, and the milestones remained unconquered.

'Tom,' said Goodchild, 'the sun is getting low. Up, and let us go forward!'

'Nay,' quoth Thomas Idle, 'I have not done with Annie Laurie yet.' And he proceeded with that idle but popular ballad, to the effect that for the bonnie young person of that name he would 'lay him doon and dee'– equivalent, in prose, to lay him down and die.

'What an ass that fellow was!' cried Goodchild, with the bitter emphasis of contempt.

'Which fellow?' asked Thomas Idle.

'The fellow in your song. Lay him doon and dee! Finely he'd show off before the girl by doing THAT. A sniveller! Why couldn't he get up, and punch somebody's head!'

'Whose?' asked Thomas Idle.

'Anybody's. Everybody's would be better than nobody's! If I fell into that state of mind about a girl, do you think I'd lay me doon and dee? No, sir,' proceeded Goodchild, with a disparaging assumption of the Scottish accent, 'I'd get me oop and peetch into somebody. Wouldn't you?'

'I wouldn't have anything to do with her,' yawned Thomas Idle. 'Why should I take the trouble?'

'It's no trouble, Tom, to fall in love,' said Goodchild, shaking his head.

'It's trouble enough to fall out of it, once you're in it,' retorted Tom. 'So I keep out of it altogether. It would be better for you, if you did the same.'

Mr. Goodchild, who is always in love with somebody, and not unfrequently with several objects at once, made no reply. He heaved a sigh of the kind which is termed by the lower orders 'a bellowser,' and then, heaving Mr. Idle on his feet (who was not half so heavy as the sigh), urged him northward.

These two had sent their personal baggage on by train: only retaining each a knapsack. Idle now applied himself to constantly regretting the train, to tracking it through the intricacies of Bradshaw's Guide, and finding out where it is now – and where now – and where now – and to asking what was the use of walking, when you could ride at such a pace as that. Was it to see the country? If that was the object, look at it out of the carriage windows. There was a great deal more of it to be seen there than here. Besides, who wanted to see the country? Nobody. And again, whoever did walk? Nobody. Fellows set off to walk, but they never did it. They came back and said they did, but they didn't. Then why should he walk? He wouldn't walk. He swore it by this milestone!

It was the fifth from London, so far had they penetrated into the North. Submitting to the powerful chain of argument, Goodchild proposed a return to the Metropolis, and a falling back upon Euston Square Terminus. Thomas assented with alacrity, and so they walked down into the North by the next morning's express, and carried their knapsacks in the luggage-van.

It was like all other expresses, as every express is and must be. It bore through the harvest country a smell like a large washing-day, and a sharp issue of steam as from a huge brazen tea-urn. The greatest power in nature and art combined, it yet glided over dangerous heights in the sight of people looking up from fields and roads, as smoothly and unreally as a light miniature plaything. Now, the engine shrieked in hysterics of such intensity, that it seemed desirable that the men who had her in charge should hold her feet, slap her hands, and bring her to; now, burrowed into tunnels with a stubborn and undemonstrative energy so confusing that the train seemed to be flying back into leagues of darkness. Here, were station after station, swallowed up by the express without stopping; here, stations where it fired itself in like a volley of cannonballs, swooped away four country-people with nosegays, and three men of business with portmanteaus, and fired itself off again, bang, bang, bang! At long intervals were uncomfortable refreshment-rooms, made more uncomfortable by the scorn of Beauty towards Beast, the public (but to whom she never relented, as Beauty did in the story, towards the other Beast), and where sensitive stomachs were fed, with a contemptuous sharpness occasioning indigestion. Here, again, were stations with nothing going but a bell, and wonderful wooden razors set aloft on great posts, shaving the air. In these fields, the horses, sheep, and cattle were well used to the thundering meteor, and didn't mind; in those, they were all set scampering together, and a herd of pigs scoured after them. The pastoral country darkened, became coaly, became smoky, became infernal, got better, got worse, improved again, grew rugged, turned romantic; was a wood, a stream, a chain of hills, a gorge, a moor, a cathedral town, a fortified place, a waste. Now, miserable black dwellings, a black canal, and sick black towers of chimneys; now, a trim garden, where the flowers were bright and fair; now, a wilderness of hideous altars all ablaze; now, the water meadows with their fairy rings; now, the mangy patch of unlet building ground outside the stagnant town, with the larger ring where the Circus was last week. The temperature changed, the dialect changed, the people changed, faces got sharper, manner got shorter, eyes got shrewder and harder; yet all so quickly, that the spruce guard in the London uniform and silver lace, had not yet rumpled his shirt-collar, delivered half the dispatches in his shiny little pouch, or read his newspaper.

Carlisle! Idle and Goodchild had got to Carlisle. It looked congenially and delightfully idle.

Something in the way of public amusement had happened last month, and something else was going to happen before Christmas; and, in the meantime there was a lecture on India for those who liked it – which Idle and Goodchild did not. Likewise, by those who liked them, there were impressions to be bought of all the vapid prints, going and gone, and of nearly all the vapid books. For those who wanted to put anything in missionary boxes, here were the boxes. For those who wanted the Reverend Mr. Podgers (artist's proofs, thirty shillings), here was Mr. Podgers to any amount. Not less gracious and abundant, Mr. Codgers also of the vineyard, but opposed to Mr. Podgers, brotherly tooth and nail. Here, were guidebooks to the neighbouring antiquities, and eke the Lake country, in several dry and husky sorts; here, many physically and morally impossible heads of both sexes, for young ladies to copy, in the exercise of the art of drawing; here, further, a large impression of MR. SPURGEON, solid as to the flesh, not to say even something gross. The working young men of Carlisle were drawn up, with their hands in their pockets, across the pavements, four and six abreast, and appeared (much to the satisfaction of Mr. Idle) to have nothing else to do. The working and growing young women of Carlisle, from the age of twelve upwards, promenaded the streets in the cool of the evening, and rallied the said young men. Sometimes the young men rallied the young women, as in the case of a group gathered round an accordion-player, from among whom a young man advanced behind a young woman for whom he appeared to have a tenderness, and hinted to her that he was there and playful, by giving her (he wore clogs) a kick.

On market morning, Carlisle woke up amazingly, and became (to the two Idle Apprentices) disagreeably and reproachfully busy. There were its cattle market, its sheep market, and its pig market down by the river, with rawboned and shock-headed Rob Roys hiding their Lowland dresses beneath heavy plaids, prowling in and out among the animals, and flavouring the air with fumes of whiskey. There was its corn market down the main street, with hum of chaffering over open sacks. There was its general market in the street too, with heather brooms on which the purple flower still flourished, and heather baskets primitive and fresh to behold. With women trying on clogs and caps at open stalls, and 'Bible stalls' adjoining. With 'Doctor Mantle's Dispensary for the cure of all Human Maladies and no charge for advice,' and with Doctor Mantle's 'Laboratory of Medical, Chemical, and Botanical Science'– both healing institutions established on one pair of trestles, one board, and one sunblind. With the renowned phrenologist from London, begging to be favoured (at sixpence each) with the company of clients of both sexes, to whom, on examination of their heads, he would make revelations 'enabling him or her to know themselves.' Through all these bargains and blessings, the recruiting-sergeant watchfully elbowed his way, a thread of War in the peaceful skein. Likewise on the walls were printed hints that the Oxford Blues might not be indisposed to hear of a few fine active young men; and that whereas the standard of that distinguished corps is full six feet, 'growing lads of five feet eleven' need not absolutely despair of being accepted.

Scenting the morning air more pleasantly than the buried majesty of Denmark did, Messrs. Idle and Goodchild rode away from Carlisle at eight o'clock one forenoon, bound for the village of Hesket, Newmarket, some fourteen miles distant. Goodchild (who had already begun to doubt whether he was idle: as his way always is when he has nothing to do) had read of a certain black old Cumberland hill or mountain, called Carrock, or Carrock Fell; and had arrived at the conclusion that it would be the culminating triumph of Idleness to ascend the same. Thomas Idle, dwelling on the pains inseparable from that achievement, had expressed the strongest doubts of the expediency, and even of the sanity, of the enterprise; but Goodchild had carried his point, and they rode away.

Up hill and down hill, and twisting to the right, and twisting to the left, and with old Skiddaw (who has vaunted himself a great deal more than his merits deserve; but that is rather the way of the Lake country), dodging the apprentices in a picturesque and pleasant manner. Good, weatherproof, warm, pleasant houses, well white-limed, scantily dotting the road. Clean children coming out to look, carrying other clean children as big as themselves. Harvest still lying out and much rained upon; here and there, harvest still unreaped. Well-cultivated gardens attached to the cottages, with plenty of produce forced out of their hard soil. Lonely nooks, and wild; but people can be born, and married, and buried in such nooks, and can live and love, and be loved, there as elsewhere, thank God! (Mr. Good-child's remark.) By-and-by, the village. Black, coarse-stoned, rough-windowed houses; some with outer staircases, like Swiss houses; a sinuous and stony gutter winding up hill and round the corner, by way of street. All the children running out directly. Women pausing in washing, to peep from doorways and very little windows. Such were the observations of Messrs. Idle and Goodchild, as their con-veyance stopped at the village shoemaker's. Old Carrock gloomed down upon it all in a very ill-tempered state; and rain was beginning.

The village shoemaker declined to have any-thing to do with Carrock. No visitors went up Carrock. No visitors came there at all. Aa' the world ganged awa' yon. The driver appealed to the Innkeeper. The Innkeeper had two men working in the fields, and one of them should be called in, to go up Carrock as guide. Messrs. Idle and Goodchild, highly approving, entered the Innkeeper's house, to drink whiskey and eat oatcake.

The Innkeeper was not idle enough – was not idle at all, which was a great fault in him – but was a fine specimen of a north-country man, or any kind of man. He had a ruddy cheek, a bright eye, a well-knit frame, an immense hand, a cheery, outspeaking voice, and a straight, bright, broad look. He had a drawing-room, too, upstairs, which was worth a visit to the Cumberland Fells. (This was Mr. Francis Goodchild's opinion, in which Mr. Thomas Idle did not concur.)

The ceiling of this drawing-room was so crossed and recrossed by beams of unequal lengths, radiating from a centre, in a corner, that it looked like a broken starfish. The room was comfortably and solidly furnished with good mahogany and horsehair. It had a snug fireside, and a couple of well-curtained windows, looking out upon the wild country behind the house. What it most developed was, an unexpected taste for little ornaments and nick-nacks, of which it contained a most surprising number. They were not very various, consisting in great part of waxen babies with their limbs more or less mutilated, appealing on one leg to the parental affections from under little cupping glasses; but, Uncle Tom was there, in crockery, receiving theological instructions from Miss Eva, who grew out of his side like a wen, in an exceedingly rough state of profile propagandism. Engravings of Mr. Hunt's country boy, before and after his pie, were on the wall, divided by a highly-coloured nautical piece, the subject of which had all her colours (and more) flying, and was making great way through a sea of a regular pattern, like a lady's collar. A benevolent, elderly gentleman of the last century, with a powdered head, kept guard, in oil and varnish, over a most perplexing piece of furniture on a table; in appearance between a driving seat and an angular knife-box, but, when opened, a musical instrument of tinkling wires, exactly like David's harp packed for travelling. Everything became a nick-nack in this curious room. The copper teakettle, burnished up to the highest point of glory, took his station on a stand of his own at the greatest possible distance from the fireplace, and said: 'By your leave, not a kettle, but a bijou.' The Staffordshire-ware butter-dish with the cover on, got upon a little round occasional table in a window, with a worked top, and announced itself to the two chairs accidentally placed there, as an aid to polite conversation, a graceful trifle in china to be chatted over by callers, as they airily trifled away the visiting moments of a butterfly existence, in that rugged old village on the Cumberland Fells. The very footstool could not keep the floor, but got upon a sofa, and there-from proclaimed itself, in high relief of white and liver-coloured wool, a favourite spaniel coiled up for repose. Though, truly, in spite of its bright glass eyes, the spaniel was the least successful assumption in the collection: being perfectly flat, and dismally suggestive of a recent mistake in sitting down on the part of some corpulent member of the family.

There were books, too, in this room; books on the table, books on the chimneypiece, books in an open press in the corner. Fielding was there, and Smollett was there, and Steele and Addison were there, in dispersed volumes; and there were tales of those who go down to the sea in ships, for windy nights; and there was really a choice of good books for rainy days or fine. It was so very pleasant to see these things in such a lonesome by-place – so very agreeable to find these evidences of a taste, however homely, that went beyond the beautiful cleanliness and trimness of the house – so fanciful to imagine what a wonder a room must be to the little children born in the gloomy village – what grand impressions of it those of them who became wanderers over the earth would carry away; and how, at distant ends of the world, some old voyagers would die, cherishing the belief that the finest apartment known to men was once in the Hesket-Newmarket Inn, in rare old Cumberland – it was such a charmingly lazy pursuit to entertain these rambling thoughts over the choice oatcake and the genial whiskey, that Mr. Idle and Mr. Goodchild never asked themselves how it came to pass that the men in the fields were never heard of more, how the stalwart landlord replaced them without explanation, how his dogcart came to be waiting at the door, and how everything was arranged without the least arrangement for climbing to old Carrock's shoulders, and standing on his head.

Without a word of inquiry, therefore, the Two Idle Apprentices drifted out resignedly into a fine, soft, close, drowsy, penetrating rain; got into the landlord's light dogcart, and rattled off through the village for the foot of Carrock. The journey at the outset was not remarkable. The Cumberland road went up and down like all other roads; the Cumberland curs burst out from backs of cottages and barked like other curs, and the Cumberland peasantry stared after the dogcart amazedly, as long as it was in sight, like the rest of their race. The approach to the foot of the mountain resembled the approaches to the feet of most other mountains all over the world. The cultivation gradually ceased, the trees grew gradually rare, the road became gradually rougher, and the sides of the mountain looked gradually more and more lofty, and more and more difficult to get up. The dogcart was left at a lonely Farmhouse. The landlord borrowed a large umbrella, and, assuming in an instant the character of the most cheerful and adventurous of guides, led the way to the ascent. Mr. Goodchild looked eagerly at the top of the mountain, and, feeling apparently that he was now going to be very lazy indeed, shone all over wonderfully to the eye, under the influence of the contentment within and the moisture without. Only in the bosom of Mr. Thomas Idle did Despondency now hold her gloomy state. He kept it a secret; but he would have given a very handsome sum, when the ascent began, to have been back again at the inn. The sides of Carrock looked fearfully steep, and the top of Carrock was hidden in mist. The rain was falling faster and faster. The knees of Mr. Idle – always weak on walking excursions – shivered and shook with fear and damp. The wet was already penetrating through the young man's outer coat to a brand-new shooting-jacket, for which he had reluctantly paid the large sum of two guineas on leaving town; he had no stimulating refreshment about him but a small packet of clammy gingerbread nuts; he had nobody to give him an arm, nobody to push him gently behind, nobody to pull him up tenderly in front, nobody to speak to who really felt the difficulties of the ascent, the dampness of the rain, the denseness of the mist, and the unutterable folly of climbing, undriven, up any steep place in the world, when there is level ground within reach to walk on instead. Was it for this that Thomas had left London? London, where there are nice short walks in level public gardens, with benches of repose set up at convenient distances for weary travellers – London, where rugged stone is humanely pounded into little lumps for the road, and intelligently shaped into smooth slabs for the pavement! No! it was not for the laborious ascent of the crags of Carrock that Idle had left his native city, and travelled to Cumberland. Never did he feel more disastrously convinced that he had committed a very grave error in judgment than when he found himself standing in the rain at the bottom of a steep mountain, and knew that the responsibility rested on his weak shoulders of actually getting to the top of it.

The honest landlord went first, the beaming Goodchild followed, the mournful Idle brought up the rear. From time to time, the two foremost members of the expedition changed places in the order of march; but the rearguard never altered his position. Up the mountain or down the mountain, in the water or out of it, over the rocks, through the bogs, skirting the heather, Mr. Thomas Idle was always the last, and was always the man who had to be looked after and waited for. At first the ascent was delusively easy, the sides of the mountain sloped gradually, and the material of which they were composed was a soft spongy turf, very tender and pleasant to walk upon. After a hundred yards or so, however, the verdant scene and the easy slope disappeared, and the rocks began. Not noble, massive rocks, standing upright, keeping a certain regularity in their positions, and possessing, now and then, flat tops to sit upon, but little irritating, comfortless rocks, littered about anyhow, by Nature; treacherous, disheartening rocks of all sorts of small shapes and small sizes, bruisers of tender toes and trippers-up of wavering feet. When these impediments were passed, heather and slough followed. Here the steepness of the ascent was slightly mitigated; and here the exploring party of three turned round to look at the view below them. The scene of the moorland

and the fields was like a feeble water-colour drawing half sponged out. The mist was darkening, the rain was thickening, the trees were dotted about like spots of faint shadow, the division-lines which mapped out the fields were all getting blurred together, and the lonely Farmhouse where the dogcart had been left, loomed spectral in the grey light like the last human dwelling at the end of the habitable world. Was this a sight worth climbing to see? Surely – surely not!

Up again – for the top of Carrock is not reached yet. The landlord, just as good-tempered and obliging as he was at the bottom of the mountain. Mr. Goodchild brighter in the eyes and rosier in the face than ever; full of cheerful remarks and apt quotations; and walking with a springiness of step wonderful to behold. Mr. Idle, farther and farther in the rear, with the water squeaking in the toes of his boots, with his two-guinea shooting-jacket clinging damply to his aching sides, with his overcoat so full of rain, and standing out so pyramidically stiff, in consequence, from his shoulders downwards, that he felt as if he was walking in a gigantic extinguisher – the despairing spirit within him representing but too aptly the candle that had just been put out. Up and up and up again, till a ridge is reached and the outer edge of the mist on the summit of Carrock is darkly and drizzingly near. Is this the top? No, nothing like the top. It is an aggravating peculiarity of all mountains, that, although they have only one top when they are seen (as they ought always to be seen) from below, they turn out to have a perfect eruption of false tops whenever the traveller is sufficiently ill-advised to go out of his way for the purpose of ascending them. Carrock is but a trumpery little mountain of fifteen hundred feet, and it presumes to have false tops, and even precipices, as if it were Mont Blanc. No matter; Goodchild enjoys it, and will go on; and Idle, who is afraid of being left behind by himself, must follow. On entering the edge of the mist, the landlord stops, and says he hopes that it will not get any thicker. It is twenty years since he last ascended Carrock, and it is barely possible, if the mist increases, that the party may be lost on the mountain. Goodchild hears this dreadful intimation, and is not in the least impressed by it. He marches for the top that is never to be found, as if he was the Wandering Jew, bound to go on for ever, in defiance of everything. The landlord faithfully accompanies him. The two, to the dim eye of Idle, far below, look in the exaggerative mist, like a pair of friendly giants, mounting the steps of some invisible castle together. Up and up, and then down a little, and then up, and then along a strip of level ground, and then up again. The wind, a wind unknown in the happy valley, blows keen and strong; the rain-mist gets impenetrable; a dreary little cairn of stones appears. The landlord adds one to the heap, first walking all round the cairn as if he were about to perform an incantation, then dropping the stone on to the top of the heap with the gesture of a magician adding an ingredient to a cauldron in full bubble. Goodchild sits down by the cairn as if it was his study-table at home; Idle, drenched and panting, stands up with his back to the wind, ascertains distinctly that this is the top at last, looks round with all the little curiosity that is left in him, and gets, in return, a magnificent view of – Nothing!

The effect of this sublime spectacle on the minds of the exploring party is a little injured by the nature of the direct conclusion to which the sight of it points – the said conclusion being that the mountain mist has actually gathered round them, as the landlord feared it would. It now becomes imperatively necessary to settle the exact situation of the Farmhouse in the valley at which the dogcart has been left, before the travellers attempt to descend. While the landlord is endeavouring to make this discovery in his own way, Mr. Goodchild plunges his hand under his wet coat, draws out a little red morocco-case, opens it, and displays to the view of his companions a neat pocket-compass. The north is found, the point at which the Farmhouse is situated is settled, and the descent begins. After a little downward walking, Idle (behind as usual) sees his fellow-travellers turn aside sharply – tries to follow them – loses them in the mist – is shouted after, waited for, recovered – and then finds that a halt has been ordered, partly on his account, partly for the purpose of again consulting the compass.

The point in debate is settled as before between Goodchild and the landlord, and the expedition moves on, not down the mountain, but marching straight forward round the slope of it. The difficulty of following this new route is acutely felt by Thomas Idle. He finds the hardship of walking at all greatly increased by the fatigue of moving his feet straight forward along the side of a slope, when their natural tendency, at every step, is to turn off at a right angle, and go straight down the declivity. Let the reader imagine himself to be walking along the roof of a barn, instead of up or down it, and he will have an exact idea of the pedestrian difficulty in which the travellers had now involved themselves. In ten minutes more Idle was lost in the distance again, was shouted for, waited for, recovered as before; found Goodchild repeating his observation of the compass, and remonstrated warmly against the sideway route that his companions persisted in following. It appeared to the uninstructed mind of Thomas that when three men want to get to the bottom of a mountain, their business is to walk down it; and he put this view of the case, not only with emphasis, but even with some irritability. He was answered from the scientific eminence of the compass on which his companions were mounted, that there was a frightful chasm somewhere near the foot of Carrock, called The Black Arches, into which the travellers were sure to march in the mist, if they risked continuing the descent from the place where they had now halted. Idle received this answer with the silent respect which was due to the commanders of the expedition, and followed along the roof of the barn, or rather the side of the mountain, reflecting upon the assurance which he received on starting again, that the object of the party was only to gain 'a certain point,' and, this haven attained, to continue the descent afterwards until the foot of Carrock was reached. Though quite unexceptionable as an abstract form of expression, the phrase 'a certain point' has the disadvantage of sounding rather vaguely when it is pronounced on unknown ground, under a canopy of mist much thicker than a London fog. Nevertheless, after the compass, this phrase was all the clue the party had to hold by, and Idle clung to the extreme end of it as hopefully as he could.

More sideway walking, thicker and thicker mist, all sorts of points reached except the 'certain point;' third loss of Idle, third shouts for him, third recovery of him, third consultation of compass. Mr. Goodchild draws it tenderly from his pocket, and prepares to adjust it on a stone. Something falls on the turf – it is the glass. Something else drops immediately after – it is the needle. The compass is broken, and the exploring party is lost!

It is the practice of the English portion of the human race to receive all great disasters in dead silence. Mr. Goodchild restored the useless compass to his pocket without saying a word, Mr. Idle looked at the landlord, and the landlord looked at Mr. Idle. There was nothing for it now but to go on blindfold, and trust to the chapter of chances. Accordingly, the lost travellers moved forward, still walking round the slope of the mountain, still desperately resolved to avoid the Black Arches, and to succeed in reaching the 'certain point.'

A quarter of an hour brought them to the brink of a ravine, at the bottom of which there flowed a muddy little stream. Here another halt was called, and another consultation took place. The landlord, still clinging pertinaciously to the idea of reaching the 'point,' voted for crossing the ravine, and going on round the slope of the mountain. Mr. Goodchild, to the great relief of his fellow-traveller, took another view of the case, and backed Mr. Idle's proposal to descend Carrock at once, at any hazard – the rather as the running stream was a sure guide to follow from the mountain to the valley. Accordingly, the party descended to the rugged and stony banks of the stream; and here again Thomas lost ground sadly, and fell far behind his travelling companions. Not much more than six weeks had elapsed since he had sprained one of his ankles, and he began to feel this same ankle getting rather weak when he found himself among the stones that were strewn about the running water. Goodchild and the landlord were getting farther and farther ahead of him. He saw them cross the stream and disappear round a projection on its banks. He heard them shout the moment after as a signal that they had halted and were waiting for him. Answering the shout, he mended his pace, crossed the stream where they had crossed it, and was within one step of the opposite bank, when his foot slipped on a wet stone, his weak ankle gave a twist outwards, a hot, rending, tearing pain ran through it at the same moment, and down fell the idlest of the Two Idle Apprentices, crippled in an instant.

The situation was now, in plain terms, one of absolute danger. There lay Mr. Idle writhing with pain, there was the mist as thick as ever, there was the landlord as completely lost as the strangers whom he was conducting, and there was the compass broken in Goodchild's pocket. To leave the wretched Thomas on unknown ground was plainly impossible; and to get him to walk with a badly sprained ankle seemed equally out of the question. However, Goodchild (brought back by his cry for help) bandaged the ankle with a pocket-handkerchief, and assisted by the landlord, raised the crippled Apprentice to his legs, offered him a shoulder to lean on, and exhorted him for the sake of the whole party to try if he could walk. Thomas, assisted by the shoulder on one side, and a stick on the other, did try, with what pain and difficulty those only can imagine who have sprained an ankle and have had to tread on it afterwards. At a pace adapted to the feeble hobbling of a newly-lamed man, the lost party moved on, perfectly ignorant whether they were on the right side of the mountain or the wrong, and equally uncertain how long Idle would be able to contend with the pain in his ankle, before he gave in altogether and fell down again, unable to stir another step.

Slowly and more slowly, as the clog of crippled Thomas weighed heavily and more heavily on the march of the expedition, the lost travellers followed the windings of the stream, till they came to a faintly-marked cart-track, branching off nearly at right angles, to the left. After a little consultation it was resolved to follow this dim vestige of a road in the hope that it might lead to some farm or cottage, at which Idle could be left in safety. It was now getting on towards the afternoon, and it was fast becoming more than doubtful whether the party, delayed in their progress as they now were, might not be overtaken by the darkness before the right route was found, and be condemned to pass the night on the mountain, without bit or drop to comfort them, in their wet clothes.

The cart-track grew fainter and fainter, until it was washed out altogether by another little stream, dark, turbulent, and rapid. The landlord suggested, judging by the colour of the water, that it must be flowing from one of the lead mines in the neighbourhood of Carrock; and the travellers accordingly kept by the stream for a little while, in the hope of possibly wandering towards help in that way. After walking forward about two hundred yards, they came upon a mine indeed, but a mine, exhausted and abandoned; a dismal, ruinous place, with nothing but the wreck of its works and buildings left to speak for it. Here, there were a few sheep feeding. The landlord looked at them earnestly, thought he recognised the marks on them – then thought he did not – finally gave up the sheep in despair – and walked on just as ignorant of the whereabouts of the party as ever.

The march in the dark, literally as well as metaphorically in the dark, had now been continued for three-quarters of an hour from the time when the crippled Apprentice had met with his accident. Mr. Idle, with all the will to conquer the pain in his ankle, and to hobble on, found the power rapidly failing him, and felt that another ten minutes at most would find him at the end of his last physical resources. He had just made up his mind on this point, and was about to communicate the dismal result of his reflections to his companions, when the mist suddenly bright-ened, and begun to lift straight ahead. In another minute, the landlord, who was in advance, proclaimed that he saw a tree. Before long, other trees appeared – then a cottage – then a house beyond the cottage, and a familiar line of road rising behind it. Last of all, Carrock itself loomed darkly into view, far away to the right hand. The party had not only got down the mountain without knowing how, but had wandered away from it in the mist, without knowing why – away, far down on the very moor by which they had approached the base of Carrock that morning.

The happy lifting of the mist, and the still happier discovery that the travellers had groped their way, though by a very roundabout direction, to within a mile or so of the part of the valley in which the Farmhouse was situated, restored Mr. Idle's sinking spirits and reanimated his failing strength. While the landlord ran off to get the dogcart, Thomas was assisted by Goodchild to the cottage which had been the first building seen when the darkness brightened, and was propped up against the garden wall, like an artist's lay figure waiting to be forwarded, until the dogcart should arrive from the Farmhouse below. In due time – and a very long time it seemed to Mr. Idle – the rattle of wheels was heard, and the crippled Apprentice was lifted into the seat. As the dogcart was driven back to the inn, the landlord related an anecdote which he had just heard at the Farmhouse, of an unhappy man who had been lost, like his two guests and himself, on Carrock; who had passed the night there alone; who had been found the next morning, 'scared and starved;' and who never went out afterwards, except on his way to the grave. Mr. Idle heard this sad story, and derived at least one useful impression from it. Bad as the pain in his ankle was, he contrived to bear it patiently, for he felt grateful that a worse accident had not befallen him in the wilds of Carrock.

CHAPTER II

The dogcart, with Mr. Thomas Idle and his ankle on the hanging seat behind, Mr. Francis Goodchild and the Innkeeper in front, and the rain in spouts and splashes everywhere, made the best of its way back to the little inn; the broken moor country looking like miles upon miles of Pre-Adamite sop, or the ruins of some enormous jorum of antediluvian toast-and-water. The trees dripped; the eaves of the scattered cottages dripped; the barren stone walls dividing the land, dripped; the yelping dogs dripped; carts and waggons under ill-roofed penthouses, dripped; melancholy cocks and hens perching on their shafts, or seeking shelter underneath them, dripped; Mr. Goodchild dripped; Thomas Idle dripped; the innkeeper dripped; the mare dripped; the vast curtains of mist and cloud passed before the shadowy forms of the hills, streamed water as they were drawn across the landscape. Down such steep pitches that the mare seemed to be trotting on her head, and up such steep pitches that she seemed to have a supplementary leg in her tail, the dogcart jolted and tilted back to the village. It was too wet for the women to look out, it was too wet even for the children to look out; all the doors and windows were closed, and the only sign of life or motion was in the rain-punctured puddles.

Whiskey and oil to Thomas Idle's ankle, and whiskey without oil to Francis Goodchild's stomach, produced an agreeable change in the systems of both; soothing Mr. Idle's pain, which was sharp before, and sweetening Mr. Goodchild's temper, which was sweet before. Portmanteaus being then opened and clothes changed, Mr. Goodchild, through having no change of outer garments but broadcloth and velvet, suddenly became a magnificent portent in the Innkeeper's house, a shining frontispiece to the fashions for the month, and a frightful anomaly in the Cumberland village.

Greatly ashamed of his splendid appearance, the conscious Goodchild quenched it as much as possible, in the shadow of Thomas Idle's ankle, and in a corner of the little covered carriage that started with them for Wigton – a most desirable carriage for any country, except for its having a flat roof and no sides; which caused the plumps of rain accumulating on the roof to play vigorous games of bagatelle into the interior all the way, and to score immensely. It was comfortable to see how the people coming back in open carts from Wigton market made no more of the rain than if it were sunshine; how the Wigton policeman taking a country walk of half-a-dozen miles (apparently for pleasure), in resplendent uniform, accepted saturation as his normal state; how clerks and schoolmasters in black, loitered along the road without umbrellas, getting varnished at every step; how the Cumberland girls, coming out to look after the Cumberland cows, shook the rain from their eyelashes and laughed it away; and how the rain continued to fall upon all, as it only does fall in hill countries.

Wigton market was over, and its bare booths were smoking with rain all down the street. Mr. Thomas Idle, melodramatically carried to the inn's first floor, and laid upon three chairs (he should have had the sofa, if there had been one), Mr. Goodchild went to the window to take an observation of Wigton, and report what he saw to his disabled companion.

'Brother Francis, brother Francis,' cried Thomas Idle, 'What do you see from the turret?'

'I see,' said Brother Francis, 'what I hope and believe to be one of the most dismal places ever seen by eyes. I see the houses with their roofs of dull black, their stained fronts, and their dark-rimmed windows, looking as if they were all in mourning. As every little puff of wind comes down the street, I see a perfect train of rain let off along the wooden stalls in the marketplace and exploded against me. I see a very big gas lamp in the centre which I know, by a secret instinct, will not be lighted tonight. I see a pump, with a trivet underneath its spout whereon to stand the vessels that are brought to be filled with water. I see a man come to pump, and he pumps very hard, but no water follows, and he strolls empty away.'

'Brother Francis, brother Francis,' cried Thomas Idle, 'what more do you see from the turret, besides the man and the pump, and the trivet and the houses all in mourning and the rain?'

'I see,' said Brother Francis, 'one, two, three, four, five, linen-drapers' shops in front of me. I see a linen-draper's shop next door to the right – and there are five more linen-drapers' shops down the corner to the left. Eleven homicidal linen-drapers' shops within a short stone's throw, each with its hands at the throats of all the rest! Over the small first-floor of one of these linen-drapers' shops appears the wonderful inscription, BANK.'

'Brother Francis, brother Francis,' cried Thomas Idle, 'what more do you see from the turret, besides the eleven homicidal linen-drapers' shops, and the wonderful inscription, "Bank,"– on the small first-floor, and the man and the pump and the trivet and the houses all in mourning and the rain?'

'I see,' said Brother Francis, 'the depository for Christian Knowledge, and through the dark vapour I think I again make out Mr. Spurgeon looming heavily. Her Majesty the Queen, God bless her, printed in colours, I am sure I see. I see the ILLUSTRATED LONDON NEWS of several years ago, and I see a sweetmeat shop – which the proprietor calls a "Salt Warehouse" – with one small female child in a cotton bonnet looking in on tiptoe, oblivious of rain. And I see a watchmaker's with only three great pale watches of a dull metal hanging in his window, each in a separate pane.'

'Brother Francis, brother Francis,' cried Thomas Idle, 'what more do you see of Wigton, besides these objects, and the man and the pump and the trivet and the houses all in mourning and the rain?'

'I see nothing more,' said Brother Francis, 'and there is nothing more to see, except the curlpaper bill of the theatre, which was opened and shut last week (the manager's family played all the parts), and the short, square, chinky omnibus that goes to the railway, and leads too rattling a life over the stones to hold together long. O yes! Now, I see two men with their hands in their pockets and their backs towards me.'

'Brother Francis, brother Francis,' cried Thomas Idle, 'what do you make out from the turret, of the expression of the two men with their hands in their pockets and their backs towards you?'

'They are mysterious men,' said Brother Francis, 'with inscrutable backs. They keep their backs towards me with persistency. If one turns an inch in any direction, the other turns an inch in the same direction, and no more. They turn very stiffly, on a very little pivot, in the middle of the marketplace. Their appearance is partly of a mining, partly of a ploughing, partly of a stable, character. They are looking at nothing – very hard. Their backs are slouched, and their legs are curved with much standing about. Their pockets are loose and dog's-eared, on account of their hands being always in them. They stand to be rained upon, without any movement of impatience or dissatisfaction, and they keep so close together that an elbow of each jostles an elbow of the other, but they never speak. They spit at times, but speak not. I see it growing darker and darker, and still I see them, sole visible population of the place, standing to be rained upon with their backs towards me, and looking at nothing very hard.'

'Brother Francis, brother Francis,' cried Thomas Idle, 'before you draw down the blind of the turret and come in to have your head scorched by the hot gas, see if you can, and impart to me, something of the expression of those two amazing men.'

'The murky shadows,' said Francis Goodchild, 'are gathering fast; and the wings of evening, and the wings of coal, are folding over Wigton. Still, they look at nothing very hard, with their backs towards me. Ah! Now, they turn, and I see–'

'Brother Francis, brother Francis,' cried Thomas Idle, 'tell me quickly what you see of the two men of Wigton!'

'I see,' said Francis Goodchild, 'that they have no expression at all. And now the town goes to sleep, undazzled by the large unlighted lamp in the marketplace; and let no man wake it.'

At the close of the next day's journey, Mr. Thomas Idle's ankle became much swollen and inflamed. There are reasons which will presently explain themselves for not publicly indicating the exact direction in which that journey lay, or the place in which it ended. It was a long day's shaking of Thomas Idle over the rough roads, and a long day's getting out and going on before the horses, and fagging up hills, and scouring down hills, on the part of Mr. Goodchild, who in the fatigues of such labours congratulated himself on attaining a high point of idleness. It was at a little town, still in Cumberland, that they halted for the night – a very little town, with the purple and brown moor close upon its one street; a curious little ancient market-cross set up in the midst of it; and the town itself looking much as if it were a collection of great stones piled on end by the Druids long ago, which a few recluse people had since hollowed out for habitations.

'Is there a doctor here?' asked Mr. Goodchild, on his knee, of the motherly landlady of the little Inn: stopping in his examination of Mr. Idle's ankle, with the aid of a candle.

'Ey, my word!' said the landlady, glancing doubtfully at the ankle for herself; 'there's Doctor Speddie.'

'Is he a good Doctor?'

'Ey!' said the landlady, 'I ca' him so. A' cooms efther nae doctor that I ken. Mair nor which, a's just THE doctor heer.'

'Do you think he is at home?'

Her reply was, 'Gang awa', Jock, and bring him.'

Jock, a white-headed boy, who, under pretence of stirring up some bay salt in a basin of water for the laving of this unfortunate ankle, had greatly enjoyed himself for the last ten minutes in splashing the carpet, set off promptly. A very few minutes had elapsed when he showed the Doctor in, by tumbling against the door before him and bursting it open with his head.

'Gently, Jock, gently,' said the Doctor as he advanced with a quiet step. 'Gentlemen, a good evening. I am sorry that my presence is required here. A slight accident, I hope? A slip and a fall? Yes, yes, yes. Carrock, indeed? Hah! Does that pain you, sir? No doubt, it does. It is the great connecting ligament here, you see, that has been badly strained. Time and rest, sir! They are often the recipe in greater cases,' with a slight sigh, 'and often the recipe in small. I can send a lotion to relieve you, but we must leave the cure to time and rest.'

This he said, holding Idle's foot on his knee between his two hands, as he sat over against him. He had touched it tenderly and skilfully in explanation of what he said, and, when his careful examination was completed, softly returned it to its former horizontal position on a chair.

He spoke with a little irresolution whenever he began, but afterwards fluently. He was a tall, thin, large-boned, old gentleman, with an appearance at first sight of being hard-featured; but, at a second glance, the mild expression of his face and some particular touches of sweetness and patience about his mouth, corrected this impression and assigned his long professional rides, by day and night, in the bleak hill-weather, as the true cause of that appearance. He stooped very little, though past seventy and very grey. His dress was more like that of a clergyman than a country doctor, being a plain black suit, and a plain white neck-kerchief tied behind like a band. His black was the worse for wear, and there were darns in his coat, and his linen was a little frayed at the hems and edges. He might have been poor – it was likely enough in that out-of-the-way spot – or he might have been a little self-forgetful and eccentric. Any one could have seen directly, that he had neither wife nor child at home. He had a scholarly air with him, and that kind of considerate humanity towards others which claimed a gentle consideration for himself. Mr. Goodchild made this study of him while he was examining the limb, and as he laid it down. Mr. Goodchild wishes to add that he considers it a very good likeness.

It came out in the course of a little conversation, that Doctor Speddie was acquainted with some friends of Thomas Idle's, and had, when a young man, passed some years in Thomas Idle's birthplace on the other side of England. Certain idle labours, the fruit of Mr. Goodchild's apprenticeship, also happened to be well known to him. The lazy travellers were thus placed on a more intimate footing with the Doctor than the casual circumstances of the meeting would of themselves have established; and when Doctor Speddie rose to go home, remarking that he would send his assistant with the lotion, Francis Goodchild said that was unnecessary, for, by the Doctor's leave, he would accompany him, and bring it back. (Having done nothing to fatigue himself for a full quarter of an hour, Francis began to fear that he was not in a state of idleness.)

Doctor Speddie politely assented to the proposition of Francis Goodchild, 'as it would give him the pleasure of enjoying a few more minutes of Mr. Goodchild's society than he could otherwise have hoped for,' and they went out together into the village street. The rain had nearly ceased, the clouds had broken before a cool wind from the northeast, and stars were shining from the peaceful heights beyond them.

Doctor Speddie's house was the last house in the place. Beyond it, lay the moor, all dark and lonesome. The wind moaned in a low, dull, shivering manner round the little garden, like a houseless creature that knew the winter was coming. It was exceedingly wild and solitary. 'Roses,' said the Doctor, when Goodchild touched some wet leaves overhanging the stone porch; 'but they get cut to pieces.'

The Doctor opened the door with a key he carried, and led the way into a low but pretty ample hall with rooms on either side. The door of one of these stood open, and the Doctor entered it, with a word of welcome to his guest. It, too, was a low room, half surgery and half parlour, with shelves of books and bottles against the walls, which were of a very dark hue. There was a fire in the grate, the night being damp and chill. Leaning against the chimneypiece looking down into it, stood the Doctor's Assistant.

A man of a most remarkable appearance. Much older than Mr. Goodchild had expected, for he was at least two-and-fifty; but, that was nothing. What was startling in him was his remarkable paleness. His large black eyes, his sunken cheeks, his long and heavy iron-grey hair, his wasted hands, and even the attenuation of his figure, were at first forgotten in his extraordinary pallor. There was no vestige of colour in the man. When he turned his face, Francis Goodchild started as if a stone figure had looked round at him.

'Mr. Lorn,' said the Doctor. 'Mr. Goodchild.'

The Assistant, in a distraught way – as if he had forgotten something – as if he had forgotten everything, even to his own name and himself – acknowledged the visitor's presence, and stepped further back into the shadow of the wall behind him. But, he was so pale that his face stood out in relief again the dark wall, and really could not be hidden so.

'Mr. Goodchild's friend has met with accident, Lorn,' said Doctor Speddie. 'We want the lotion for a bad sprain.'

A pause.

'My dear fellow, you are more than usually absent tonight. The lotion for a bad sprain.'

'Ah! yes! Directly.'

He was evidently relieved to turn away, and to take his white face and his wild eyes to a table in a recess among the bottles. But, though he stood there, compounding the lotion with his back towards them, Goodchild could not, for many moments, withdraw his gaze from the man. When he at length did so, he found the

Doctor observing him, with some trouble in his face. 'He is absent,' explained the Doctor, in a low voice. 'Always absent. Very absent.'

'Is he ill?'

'No, not ill.'

'Unhappy?'

'I have my suspicions that he was,' assented the Doctor, 'once.'

Francis Goodchild could not but observe that the Doctor accompanied these words with a benignant and protecting glance at their subject, in which there was much of the expression with which an attached father might have looked at a heavily afflicted son. Yet, that they were not father and son must have been plain to most eyes. The Assistant, on the other hand, turning presently to ask the Doctor some question, looked at him with a wan smile as if he were his whole reliance and sustainment in life.

It was in vain for the Doctor in his easy-chair, to try to lead the mind of Mr. Goodchild in the opposite easy-chair, away from what was before him. Let Mr. Goodchild do what he would to follow the Doctor, his eyes and thoughts reverted to the Assistant. The Doctor soon perceived it, and, after falling silent, and musing in a little perplexity, said:

'Lorn!'

'My dear Doctor.'

'Would you go to the Inn, and apply that lotion? You will show the best way of applying it, far better than Mr. Goodchild can.'

'With pleasure.'

The Assistant took his hat, and passed like a shadow to the door.

'Lorn!' said the Doctor, calling after him.

He returned.

'Mr. Goodchild will keep me company till you come home. Don't hurry. Excuse my calling you back.'

'It is not,' said the Assistant, with his former smile, 'the first time you have called me back, dear Doctor.' With those words he went away.

'Mr. Goodchild,' said Doctor Speddie, in a low voice, and with his former troubled expression of face, 'I have seen that your attention has been concentrated on my friend.'

'He fascinates me. I must apologise to you, but he has quite bewildered and mastered me.'

'I find that a lonely existence and a long secret,' said the Doctor, drawing his chair a little nearer to Mr. Goodchild's, 'become in the course of time very heavy. I will tell you something. You may make what use you will of it, under fictitious names. I know I may trust you. I am the more inclined to confidence tonight, through having been unexpectedly led back, by the current of our conversation at the Inn, to scenes in my early life. Will you please to draw a little nearer?'

Mr. Goodchild drew a little nearer, and the Doctor went on thus: speaking, for the most part, in so cautious a voice, that the wind, though it was far from high, occasionally got the better of him.

When this present nineteenth century was younger by a good many years than it is now, a certain friend of mine, named Arthur Holliday, happened to arrive in the town of Doncaster, exactly in the middle of a race-week, or, in other words, in the middle of the month of September. He was one of those reckless, rattle-pated, openhearted, and openmouthed young gentlemen, who possess the gift of familiarity in its highest perfection, and who scramble carelessly along the journey of life making friends, as the phrase is, wherever they go. His father was a rich manufacturer, and had bought landed property enough in one of the midland counties to make all the born squires in his neighbourhood thoroughly envious of him. Arthur was his only son, possessor in prospect of the great estate and the great business after his father's death; well supplied with money, and not too rigidly looked after, during his father's lifetime. Report, or scandal, whichever you please, said that the old gentleman had been rather wild in his youthful days, and that, unlike most parents, he was not disposed to be violently indignant when he found that his son took after him. This may be true or not. I myself only knew the elder Mr. Holliday when he was getting on in years; and then he was as quiet and as respectable a gentleman as ever I met with.

Well, one September, as I told you, young Arthur comes to Doncaster, having decided all of a sudden, in his harebrained way, that he would go to the races. He did not reach the town till towards the close of the evening, and he went at once to see about his dinner and bed at the principal hotel. Dinner they were ready enough to give him; but as for a bed, they laughed when he mentioned it. In the race-week at Doncaster, it is no uncommon thing for visitors who have not bespoken apartments, to pass the night in their carriages at the inn doors. As for the lower sort of strangers, I myself have often seen them, at that full time, sleeping out on the doorsteps for want of a covered place to creep under. Rich as he was, Arthur's chance of getting a night's lodging (seeing that he had not written beforehand to secure one) was more than doubtful. He tried the second hotel, and the third hotel, and two of the inferior inns after that; and was met everywhere by the same form of answer. No accommodation for the night of any sort was left. All the bright golden sovereigns in his pocket would not buy him a bed at Doncaster in the race-week.

To a young fellow of Arthur's temperament, the novelty of being turned away into the street, like a penniless vagabond, at every house where he asked for a lodging, presented itself in the light of a new and highly amusing piece of experience. He went on, with his carpetbag in his hand, applying for a bed at every place of entertainment for travellers that he could find in Doncaster, until he wandered into the outskirts of the town. By this time, the last glimmer of twilight had faded out, the moon was rising dimly in a mist, the wind was getting cold, the clouds were gathering heavily, and there was every prospect that it was soon going to rain.

The look of the night had rather a lowering effect on young Holliday's good spirits. He began to contemplate the houseless situation in which he was placed, from the serious rather than the humorous point of view; and he looked about him, for another public-house to inquire at, with something very like downright anxiety in his mind on the subject of a lodging for the night. The suburban part of the town towards which he had now strayed was hardly lighted at all, and he could see nothing of the houses as he passed them, except that they got progressively smaller and dirtier, the farther he went. Down the winding road before him shone the dull gleam of an oil lamp, the one faint, lonely light that struggled ineffectually with the foggy darkness all round him. He resolved to go on as far as this lamp, and then, if it showed him nothing in the shape of an Inn, to return to the central part of the town and to try if he could not at least secure a chair to sit down on, through the night, at one of the principal Hotels.

As he got near the lamp, he heard voices; and, walking close under it, found that it lighted the entrance to a narrow court, on the wall of which was painted a long hand in faded flesh-colour, pointing with a lean forefinger, to this inscription:–

THE TWO ROBINS.

Arthur turned into the court without hesitation, to see what The Two Robins could do for him. Four or five men were standing together round the door of the house which was at the bottom of the court, facing the entrance from the street. The men were all listening to one other man, better dressed than the rest, who was telling his audience something, in a low voice, in which they were apparently very much interested.

On entering the passage, Arthur was passed by a stranger with a knapsack in his hand, who was evidently leaving the house.

'No,' said the traveller with the knapsack, turning round and addressing himself cheerfully to a fat, sly-looking, baldheaded man, with a dirty white apron on, who had followed him down the passage. 'No, Mr. landlord, I am not easily scared by trifles; but, I don't mind confessing that I can't quite stand THAT.'

It occurred to young Holliday, the moment he heard these words, that the stranger had been asked an exorbitant price for a bed at The Two Robins; and that he was unable or unwilling to pay it. The moment his back was turned, Arthur, comfortably conscious of his own well-filled pockets, addressed himself in a great hurry, for fear any other benighted traveller should slip in and forestall him, to the sly-looking landlord with the dirty apron and the bald head.

'If you have got a bed to let,' he said, 'and if that gentleman who has just gone out won't pay your price for it, I will.'

The sly landlord looked hard at Arthur.

'Will you, sir?' he asked, in a meditative, doubtful way.

'Name your price,' said young Holliday, thinking that the landlord's hesitation sprang from some boorish distrust of him. 'Name your price, and I'll give you the money at once if you like?'

'Are you game for five shillings?' inquired the landlord, rubbing his stubbly double chin, and looking up thoughtfully at the ceiling above him.

Arthur nearly laughed in the man's face; but thinking it prudent to control himself, offered the five shillings as seriously as he could. The sly landlord held out his hand, then suddenly drew it back again.

'You're acting all fair and aboveboard by me,' he said: 'and, before I take your money, I'll do the same by you. Look here, this is how it stands. You can have a bed all to yourself for five shillings; but you can't have more than a half-share of the room it stands in. Do you see what I mean, young gentleman?'

'Of course I do,' returned Arthur, a little irritably. 'You mean that it is a double-bedded room, and that one of the beds is occupied?'

The landlord nodded his head, and rubbed his double chin harder than ever. Arthur hesitated, and mechanically moved back a step or two towards the door. The idea of sleeping in the same room with a total stranger, did not present an attractive prospect to him. He felt more than half inclined to drop his five shillings into his pocket, and to go out into the street once more.

'Is it yes, or no?' asked the landlord. 'Settle it as quick as you can, because there's lots of people wanting a bed at Doncaster tonight, besides you.'

Arthur looked towards the court, and heard the rain falling heavily in the street outside. He thought he would ask a question or two before he rashly decided on leaving the shelter of The Two Robins.

'What sort of a man is it who has got the other bed?' he inquired. 'Is he a gentleman? I mean, is he a quiet, well-behaved person?'

'The quietest man I ever came across,' said the landlord, rubbing his fat hands stealthily one over the other. 'As sober as a judge, and as regular as clockwork in his habits. It hasn't struck nine, not ten minutes ago, and he's in his bed already. I don't know whether that comes up to your notion of a quiet man: it goes a long way ahead of mine, I can tell you.'

'Is he asleep, do you think?' asked Arthur.

'I know he's asleep,' returned the landlord. 'And what's more, he's gone off so fast, that I'll warrant you don't wake him. This way, sir,' said the landlord, speaking over young Holliday's shoulder, as if he was addressing some new guest who was approaching the house.

'Here you are,' said Arthur, determined to be beforehand with the stranger, whoever he might be. 'I'll take the bed.' And he handed the five shillings to the landlord, who nodded, dropped the money carelessly into his waistcoat-pocket, and lighted the candle.

'Come up and see the room,' said the host of The Two Robins, leading the way to the staircase quite briskly, considering how fat he was.

They mounted to the second-floor of the house. The landlord half opened a door, fronting the landing, then stopped, and turned round to Arthur.

'It's a fair bargain, mind, on my side as well as on yours,' he said. 'You give me five shillings, I give you in return a clean, comfortable bed; and I warrant, beforehand, that you won't be interfered with, or annoyed in any way, by the man who sleeps in the same room as you.' Saying those words, he looked hard, for a moment, in young Holliday's face, and then led the way into the room.

It was larger and cleaner than Arthur had expected it would be. The two beds stood parallel with each other – a space of about six feet intervening between them. They were both of the same medium size, and both had the same plain white curtains, made to draw, if necessary, all round them. The occupied bed was the bed nearest the window. The curtains were all drawn round this, except the half curtain at the bottom, on the side of the bed farthest from the window. Arthur saw the feet of the sleeping man raising the scanty clothes into a sharp little eminence, as if he was lying flat on his back. He took the candle, and advanced softly to draw the curtain – stopped halfway, and listened for a moment – then turned to the landlord.

'He's a very quiet sleeper,' said Arthur.

'Yes,' said the landlord, 'very quiet.'

Young Holliday advanced with the candle, and looked in at the man cautiously.

'How pale he is!' said Arthur.

'Yes,' returned the landlord, 'pale enough, isn't he?'

Arthur looked closer at the man. The bedclothes were drawn up to his chin, and they lay perfectly still over the region of his chest. Surprised and vaguely startled, as he noticed this, Arthur stooped down closer over the stranger; looked at his ashy, parted lips; listened breathlessly for an instant; looked again at the strangely still face, and the motionless lips and chest; and turned round suddenly on the landlord, with his own cheeks as pale for the moment as the hollow cheeks of the man on the bed.

'Come here,' he whispered, under his breath. 'Come here, for God's sake! The man's not asleep – he is dead!'

'You have found that out sooner than I thought you would,' said the landlord, composedly. 'Yes, he's dead, sure enough. He died at five o'clock today.'

'How did he die? Who is he?' asked Arthur, staggered, for a moment, by the audacious coolness of the answer.

'As to who is he,' rejoined the landlord, 'I know no more about him than you do. There are his books and letters and things, all sealed up in that brown-paper parcel, for the Coroner's inquest to open tomorrow or next day. He's been here a week, paying his way fairly enough, and stopping indoors, for the most part, as if he was ailing. My girl brought him up his tea at five today; and as he was pouring of it out, he fell down in a faint, or a fit, or a compound of both, for anything I know. We could not bring him to – and I said he was dead. And the doctor couldn't bring him to – and the doctor said he was dead. And there he is. And the Coroner's inquest's coming as soon as it can. And that's as much as I know about it.'

Arthur held the candle close to the man's lips. The flame still burnt straight up, as steadily as before. There was a moment of silence; and the rain pattered drearily through it against the panes of the window.

'If you haven't got nothing more to say to me,' continued the landlord, 'I suppose I may go. You don't expect your five shillings back, do you? There's the bed I promised you, clean and comfortable. There's the man I warranted not to disturb you, quiet in this world for ever. If you're frightened to stop alone with him, that's not my look out. I've kept my part of the bargain, and I mean to keep the money. I'm not Yorkshire, myself, young gentleman; but I've lived long enough in these parts to have my wits sharpened; and I shouldn't wonder if you found out the way to brighten up yours, next time you come amongst us.' With these words, the landlord turned towards the door, and laughed to himself softly, in high satisfaction at his own sharpness.

Startled and shocked as he was, Arthur had by this time sufficiently recovered himself to feel indignant at the trick that had been played on him, and at the insolent manner in which the landlord exulted in it.

'Don't laugh,' he said sharply, 'till you are quite sure you have got the laugh against me.

You shan't have the five shillings for nothing, my man. I'll keep the bed.'

'Will you?' said the landlord. 'Then I wish you a goodnight's rest.' With that brief farewell, he went out, and shut the door after him.

A good night's rest! The words had hardly been spoken, the door had hardly been closed, before Arthur half-repented the hasty words that had just escaped him. Though not naturally oversensitive, and not wanting in courage of the moral as well as the physical sort, the presence of the dead man had an instantaneously chilling effect on his mind when he found himself alone in the room – alone, and bound by his own rash words to stay there till the next morning. An older man would have thought nothing of those words, and would have acted, without reference to them, as his calmer sense suggested. But Arthur was too young to treat the ridicule, even of his inferiors, with contempt – too young not to fear the momentary humiliation of falsifying his own foolish boast, more than he feared the trial of watching out the long night in the same chamber with the dead.

'It is but a few hours,' he thought to himself, 'and I can get away the first thing in the morning.'

He was looking towards the occupied bed as that idea passed through his mind, and the sharp, angular eminence made in the clothes by the dead man's upturned feet again caught his eye. He advanced and drew the curtains, purposely abstaining, as he did so, from looking at the face of the corpse, lest he might unnerve himself at the outset by fastening some ghastly impression of it on his mind. He drew the curtain very gently, and sighed involuntarily as he closed it. 'Poor fellow,' he said, almost as sadly as if he had known the man. 'Ah, poor fellow!'

He went next to the window. The night was black, and he could see nothing from it. The rain still pattered heavily against the glass. He inferred, from hearing it, that the window was at the back of the house; remembering that the front was sheltered from the weather by the court and the buildings over it.

While he was still standing at the window – for even the dreary rain was a relief, because of the sound it made; a relief, also, because it moved, and had some faint suggestion, in consequence, of life and companionship in it – while he was standing at the window, and looking vacantly into the black darkness outside, he heard a distant church-clock strike ten. Only ten! How was he to pass the time till the house was astir the next morning?

Under any other circumstances, he would have gone down to the public-house parlour, would have called for his grog, and would have laughed and talked with the company assembled as familiarly as if he had known them all his life.

But the very thought of whiling away the time in this manner was distasteful to him. The new situation in which he was placed seemed to have altered him to himself already. Thus far, his life had been the common, trifling, prosaic, surface-life of a prosperous young man, with no troubles to conquer, and no trials to face. He had lost no relation whom he loved, no friend whom he treasured. Till this night, what share he had of the immortal inheritance that is divided amongst us all, had laid dormant within him. Till this night, Death and he had not once met, even in thought.

He took a few turns up and down the room – then stopped. The noise made by his boots on the poorly carpeted floor, jarred on his ear. He hesitated a little, and ended by taking the boots off, and walking backwards and forwards noiselessly. All desire to sleep or to rest had left him. The bare thought of lying down on the unoccupied bed instantly drew the picture on his mind of a dreadful mimicry of the position of the dead man. Who was he? What was the story of his past life? Poor he must have been, or he would not have stopped at such a place as The Two Robins Inn – and weakened, probably, by long illness, or he could hardly have died in the manner in which the landlord had described. Poor, ill, lonely, – dead in a strange place; dead, with nobody but a stranger to pity him. A sad story: truly, on the mere face of it, a very sad story.

While these thoughts were passing through his mind, he had stopped insensibly at the window, close to which stood the foot of the bed with the closed curtains. At first he looked at it absently; then he became conscious that his eyes were fixed on it; and then, a perverse desire took possession of him to do the very thing which he had resolved not to do, up to this time – to look at the dead man.

He stretched out his hand towards the curtains; but checked himself in the very act of undrawing them, turned his back sharply on the bed, and walked towards the chimneypiece, to see what things were placed on it, and to try if he could keep the dead man out of his mind in that way.

There was a pewter inkstand on the chimney-piece, with some mildewed remains of ink in the bottle. There were two coarse china ornaments of the commonest kind; and there was a square of embossed card, dirty and flyblown, with a collection of wretched riddles printed on it, in all sorts of zigzag directions, and in variously coloured inks. He took the card, and went away, to read it, to the table on which the candle was placed; sitting down, with his back resolutely turned to the curtained bed.

He read the first riddle, the second, the third, all in one corner of the card – then turned it round impatiently to look at another. Before he could begin reading the riddles printed here, the sound of the church-clock stopped him. Eleven. He had got through an hour of the time, in the room with the dead man.

Once more he looked at the card. It was not easy to make out the letters printed on it, in consequence of the dimness of the light which the landlord had left him – a common tallow candle, furnished with a pair of heavy old-fashioned steel snuffers. Up to this time, his mind had been too much occupied to think of the light. He had left the wick of the candle unsnuffed, till it had risen higher than the flame, and had burnt into an odd penthouse shape at the top, from which morsels of the charred cotton fell off, from time to time, in little flakes. He took up the snuffers now, and trimmed the wick. The light brightened directly, and the room became less dismal.

Again he turned to the riddles; reading them doggedly and resolutely, now in one corner of the card, now in another. All his efforts, how-ever, could not fix his attention on them. He pursued his occupation mechanically, deriving no sort of impression from what he was read-ing. It was as if a shadow from the curtained bed had got between his mind and the gaily printed letters – a shadow that nothing could dispel. At last, he gave up the struggle, and threw the card from him impatiently, and took to walking softly up and down the room again.

The dead man, the dead man, the HIDDEN dead man on the bed! There was the one persistent idea still haunting him. Hidden? Was it only the body being there, or was it the body being there, concealed, that was preying on his mind? He stopped at the window, with that doubt in him; once more listening to the pattering rain, once more looking out into the black darkness.

Still the dead man! The darkness forced his mind back upon itself, and set his memory at work, reviving, with a painfully-vivid distinctness the momentary impression it had received from the first sight of the corpse. Before long the face seemed to be hovering out in the middle of the darkness, confronting him through the window, with the paleness whiter, with the dreadful dull line of light between the imperfectly-closed eyelids broader than he had seen it – with the parted lips slowly dropping farther and farther away from each other – with the features growing larger and moving closer, till they seemed to fill the window and to silence the rain, and to shut out the night.

The sound of a voice, shouting below-stairs, woke him suddenly from the dream of his own distempered fancy. He recognised it as the voice of the landlord. 'Shut up at twelve, Ben,' he heard it say. 'I'm off to bed.'

He wiped away the damp that had gathered on his forehead, reasoned with himself for a little while, and resolved to shake his mind free of the ghastly counterfeit which still clung to it, by forcing himself to confront, if it was only for a moment, the solemn reality. Without allowing himself an instant to hesitate, he parted the curtains at the foot of the bed, and looked through.

There was a sad, peaceful, white face, with the awful mystery of stillness on it, laid back upon the pillow. No stir, no change there! He only looked at it for a moment before he closed the curtains again – but that moment steadied him, calmed him, restored him – mind and body – to himself.

He returned to his old occupation of walking up and down the room; persevering in it, this time, till the clock struck again. Twelve.

As the sound of the clock-bell died away, it was succeeded by the confused noise, downstairs, of the drinkers in the taproom leaving the house. The next sound, after an interval of silence, was caused by the barring of the door, and the closing of the shutters, at the back of the Inn. Then the silence followed again, and was disturbed no more.

He was alone now – absolutely, utterly, alone with the dead man, till the next morning.

The wick of the candle wanted trimming again. He took up the snuffers – but paused suddenly on the very point of using them, and looked attentively at the candle – then back, over his shoulder, at the curtained bed – then again at the candle. It had been lighted, for the first time, to show him the way upstairs, and three parts of it, at least, were already consumed. In another hour it would be burnt out. In another hour – unless he called at once to the man who had shut up the Inn, for a fresh candle – he would be left in the dark.

Strongly as his mind had been affected since he had entered his room, his unreasonable dread of encountering ridicule, and of exposing his courage to suspicion, had not altogether lost its influence over him, even yet. He lingered irresolutely by the table, waiting till he could prevail on himself to open the door, and call, from the landing, to the man who had shut up the Inn. In his present hesitating frame of mind, it was a kind of relief to gain a few moments only by engaging in the trifling occupation of snuffing the candle. His hand trembled a little, and the snuffers were heavy and awkward to use. When he closed them on the wick, he closed them a hair's breadth too low. In an instant the candle was out, and the room was plunged in pitch darkness.

The one impression which the absence of light immediately produced on his mind, was distrust of the curtained bed – distrust which shaped itself into no distinct idea, but which was powerful enough in its very vagueness, to bind him down to his chair, to make his heart beat fast, and to set him listening intently. No sound stirred in the room but the familiar sound of the rain against the window, louder and sharper now than he had heard it yet.

Still the vague distrust, the inexpressible dread possessed him, and kept him to his chair. He had put his carpetbag on the table, when he first entered the room; and he now took the key from his pocket, reached out his hand softly, opened the bag, and groped in it for his travelling writing-case, in which he knew that there was a small store of matches. When he had got one of the matches, he waited before he struck it on the coarse wooden table, and listened intently again, without knowing why. Still there was no sound in the room but the steady, ceaseless, rattling sound of the rain.

He lighted the candle again, without another moment of delay and, on the instant of its burning up, the first object in the room that his eyes sought for was the curtained bed.

Just before the light had been put out, he had looked in that direction, and had seen no change, no disarrangement of any sort, in the folds of the closely-drawn curtains.

When he looked at the bed, now, he saw, hanging over the side of it, a long white hand.

It lay perfectly motionless, midway on the side of the bed, where the curtain at the head and the curtain at the foot met. Nothing more was visible. The clinging curtains hid everything but the long white hand.

He stood looking at it unable to stir, unable to call out; feeling nothing, knowing nothing, every faculty he possessed gathered up and lost in the one seeing faculty. How long that first panic held him he never could tell afterwards. It might have been only for a moment; it might have been for many minutes together. How he got to the bed – whether he ran to it headlong, or whether he approached it slowly – how he wrought himself up to unclose the curtains and look in, he never has remembered, and never will remember to his dying day. It is enough that he did go to the bed, and that he did look inside the curtains.

The man had moved. One of his arms was outside the clothes; his face was turned a little on the pillow; his eyelids were wide open. Changed as to position, and as to one of the features, the face was, otherwise, fearfully and wonderfully unaltered. The dead paleness and the dead quiet were on it still

One glance showed Arthur this – one glance, before he flew breathlessly to the door, and alarmed the house.

The man whom the landlord called 'Ben,' was the first to appear on the stairs. In three words, Arthur told him what had happened, and sent him for the nearest doctor.

I, who tell you this story, was then staying with a medical friend of mine, in practice at Doncaster, taking care of his patients for him, during his absence in London; and I, for the time being, was the nearest doctor. They had sent for me from the Inn, when the stranger was taken ill in the afternoon; but I was not at home, and medical assistance was sought for elsewhere. When the man from The Two Robins rang the night-bell, I was just thinking of going to bed. Naturally enough, I did not believe a word of his story about 'a dead man who had come to life again.' However, I put on my hat, armed myself with one or two bottles of restorative medicine, and ran to the Inn, expecting to find nothing more remarkable, when I got there, than a patient in a fit.

My surprise at finding that the man had spoken the literal truth was almost, if not quite, equalled by my astonishment at finding myself face to face with Arthur Holliday as soon as I entered the bedroom. It was no time then for giving or seeking explanations. We just shook hands amazedly; and then I ordered everybody but Arthur out of the room, and hurried to the man on the bed.

The kitchen fire had not been long out. There was plenty of hot water in the boiler, and plenty of flannel to be had. With these, with my medicines, and with such help as Arthur could render under my direction, I dragged the man, literally, out of the jaws of death. In less than an hour from the time when I had been called in, he was alive and talking in the bed on which he had been laid out to wait for the Coroner's inquest.

You will naturally ask me, what had been the matter with him; and I might treat you, in reply, to a long theory, plentifully sprinkled with, what the children call, hard words. I prefer telling you that, in this case, cause and effect could not be satisfactorily joined together by any theory whatever. There are mysteries in life, and the condition of it, which human science has not fathomed yet; and I candidly confess to you, that, in bringing that man back to existence, I was, morally speaking, groping haphazard in the dark. I know (from the testimony of the doctor who attended him in the afternoon) that the vital machinery, so far as its action is appreciable by our senses, had, in this case, unquestionably stopped; and I am equally certain (seeing that I recovered him) that the vital principle was not extinct. When I add, that he had suffered from a long and complicated illness, and that his whole nervous system was utterly deranged, I have told you all I really know of the physical condition of my dead-alive patient at The Two Robins Inn.

When he 'came to,' as the phrase goes, he was a startling object to look at, with his colourless face, his sunken cheeks, his wild black eyes, and his long black hair. The first question he asked me about himself, when he could speak, made me suspect that I had been called in to a man in my own profession. I mentioned to him my surmise; and he told me that I was right.

He said he had come last from Paris, where he had been attached to a hospital. That he had lately returned to England, on his way to Edinburgh, to continue his studies; that he had been taken ill on the journey; and that he had stopped to rest and recover himself at Doncaster. He did not add a word about his name, or who he was: and, of course, I did not question him on the subject. All I inquired, when he ceased speaking, was what branch of the profession he intended to follow.

'Any branch,' he said, bitterly, 'which will put bread into the mouth of a poor man.'

At this, Arthur, who had been hitherto watching him in silent curiosity, burst out impetuously in his usual good-humoured way:–

'My dear fellow!' (everybody was 'my dear fellow' with Arthur) 'now you have come to life again, don't begin by being downhearted about your prospects. I'll answer for it, I can help you to some capital thing in the medical line – or, if I can't, I know my father can.'

The medical student looked at him steadily.

'Thank you,' he said, coldly. Then added, 'May I ask who your father is?'

'He's well enough known all about this part of the country,' replied Arthur. 'He is a great manufacturer, and his name is Holliday.'

My hand was on the man's wrist during this brief conversation. The instant the name of Holliday was pronounced I felt the pulse under my fingers flutter, stop, go on suddenly with a bound, and beat afterwards, for a minute or two, at the fever rate.

'How did you come here?' asked the stranger, quickly, excitably, passionately almost.

Arthur related briefly what had happened from the time of his first taking the bed at the inn.

'I am indebted to Mr. Holliday's son then for the help that has saved my life,' said the medical student, speaking to himself, with a singular sarcasm in his voice. 'Come here!'

He held out, as he spoke, his long, white, bony, right hand.

'With all my heart,' said Arthur, taking the hand-cordially. 'I may confess it now,' he continued, laughing. 'Upon my honour, you almost frightened me out of my wits.'

The stranger did not seem to listen. His wild black eyes were fixed with a look of eager interest on Arthur's face, and his long bony fingers kept tight hold of Arthur's hand. Young Holliday, on his side, returned the gaze, amazed and puzzled by the medical student's odd language and manners. The two faces were close together; I looked at them; and, to my amazement, I was suddenly impressed by the sense of a likeness between them – not in features, or complexion, but solely in expression. It must have been a strong likeness, or I should certainly not have found it out, for I am naturally slow at detecting resemblances between faces.

'You have saved my life,' said the strange man, still looking hard in Arthur's face, still holding tightly by his hand. 'If you had been my own brother, you could not have done more for me than that.'

He laid a singularly strong emphasis on those three words 'my own brother,' and a change passed over his face as he pronounced them, – a change that no language of mine is competent to describe.

'I hope I have not done being of service to you yet,' said Arthur. 'I'll speak to my father, as soon as I get home.'

'You seem to be fond and proud of your father,' said the medical student. 'I suppose, in return, he is fond and proud of you?'

'Of course, he is!' answered Arthur, laughing. 'Is there anything wonderful in that? Isn't YOUR father fond–'

The stranger suddenly dropped young Holliday's hand, and turned his face away.

'I beg your pardon,' said Arthur. 'I hope I have not unintentionally pained you. I hope you have not lost your father.'

'I can't well lose what I have never had,' retorted the medical student, with a harsh, mocking laugh.

'What you have never had!'

The strange man suddenly caught Arthur's hand again, suddenly looked once more hard in his face.

'Yes,' he said, with a repetition of the bitter laugh. 'You have brought a poor devil back into the world, who has no business there. Do I astonish you? Well! I have a fancy of my own for telling you what men in my situation generally keep a secret. I have no name and no father. The merciful law of Society tells me I am Nobody's Son! Ask your father if he will be my father too, and help me on in life with the family name.'

Arthur looked at me, more puzzled than ever. I signed to him to say nothing, and then laid my fingers again on the man's wrist. No! In spite of the extraordinary speech that he had just made, he was not, as I had been disposed to suspect, beginning to get lightheaded. His pulse, by this time, had fallen back to a quiet, slow beat, and his skin was moist and cool. Not a symptom of fever or agitation about him.

Finding that neither of us answered him, he turned to me, and began talking of the extraordinary nature of his case, and asking my advice about the future course of medical treatment to which he ought to subject himself. I said the matter required careful thinking over, and suggested that I should submit certain prescriptions to him the next morning. He told me to write them at once, as he would, most likely, be leaving Doncaster, in the morning, before I was up. It was quite useless to represent to him the folly and danger of such a proceeding as this. He heard me politely and patiently, but held to his resolution, without offering any reasons or any explanations, and repeated to me, that if I wished to give him a chance of seeing my prescription, I must write it at once. Hearing this, Arthur volunteered the loan of a travelling writing-case, which, he said, he had with him; and, bringing it to the bed, shook the notepaper out of the pocket of the case forthwith in his usual careless way. With the paper, there fell out on the counterpane of the bed a small packet of sticking-plaster, and a little water-colour drawing of a landscape.

The medical student took up the drawing and looked at it. His eye fell on some initials neatly written, in cypher, in one corner. He started and trembled; his pale face grew whiter than ever; his wild black eyes turned on Arthur, and looked through and through him.

'A pretty drawing,' he said in a remarkably quiet tone of voice.

'Ah! and done by such a pretty girl,' said Arthur. 'Oh, such a pretty girl! I wish it was not a landscape – I wish it was a portrait of her!'

'You admire her very much?'

Arthur, half in jest, half in earnest, kissed his hand for answer.

'Love at first sight!' he said, putting the drawing away again. 'But the course of it doesn't run smooth. It's the old story. She's monopolised as usual. Trammelled by a rash engagement to some poor man who is never likely to get money enough to marry her. It was lucky I heard of it in time, or I should certainly have risked a declaration when she gave me that drawing. Here, doctor! Here is pen, ink, and paper all ready for you.'

'When she gave you that drawing? Gave it. Gave it.' He repeated the words slowly to himself, and suddenly closed his eyes. A momentary distortion passed across his face, and I saw one of his hands clutch up the bedclothes and squeeze them hard. I thought he was going to be ill again, and begged that there might be no more talking. He opened his eyes when I spoke, fixed them once more searchingly on Arthur, and said, slowly and distinctly, 'You like her, and she likes you. The poor man may die out of your way. Who can tell that she may not give you herself as well as her drawing, after all?'

Before young Holliday could answer, he turned to me, and said in a whisper, 'Now for the prescription.' From that time, though he spoke to Arthur again, he never looked at him more.

When I had written the prescription, he examined it, approved of it, and then astonished us both by abruptly wishing us good night. I offered to sit up with him, and he shook his head. Arthur offered to sit up with him, and he said, shortly, with his face turned away, 'No.' I insisted on having somebody left to watch him. He gave way when he found I was determined, and said he would accept the services of the waiter at the Inn.

'Thank you, both,' he said, as we rose to go. 'I have one last favour to ask – not of you, doctor, for I leave you to exercise your professional discretion – but of Mr. Holliday.' His eyes, while he spoke, still rested steadily on me, and never once turned towards Arthur. 'I beg that Mr. Holliday will not mention to any one – least of all to his father – the events that have occurred, and the words that have passed, in this room. I entreat him to bury me in his memory, as, but for him, I might have been buried in my grave. I cannot give my reasons for making this strange request. I can only implore him to grant it.'

His voice faltered for the first time, and he hid his face on the pillow. Arthur, completely bewildered, gave the required pledge. I took young Holliday away with me, immediately afterwards, to the house of my friend; determining to go back to the Inn, and to see the medical student again before he had left in the morning.

I returned to the Inn at eight o'clock, purposely abstaining from waking Arthur, who was sleeping off the past night's excitement on one of my friend's sofas. A suspicion had occurred to me as soon as I was alone in my bedroom, which made me resolve that Holliday and the stranger whose life he had saved should not meet again, if I could prevent it. I have already alluded to certain reports, or scandals, which I knew of, relating to the early life of Arthur's father. While I was thinking, in my bed, of what had passed at the Inn – of the change in the student's pulse when he heard the name of Holliday; of the resemblance of expression that I had discovered between his face and Arthur's; of the emphasis he had laid on those three words, 'my own brother;' and of his incomprehensible acknowledgment of his own illegitimacy – while I was thinking of these things, the reports I have mentioned suddenly flew into my mind, and linked themselves fast to the chain of my previous reflections. Something within me whispered, 'It is best that those two young men should not meet again.' I felt it before I slept; I felt it when I woke; and I went, as I told you, alone to the Inn the next morning.

I had missed my only opportunity of seeing my nameless patient again. He had been gone nearly an hour when I inquired for him.

I have now told you everything that I know for certain, in relation to the man whom I brought back to life in the double-bedded room of the Inn at Doncaster. What I have next to add is matter for inference and surmise, and is not, strictly speaking, matter of fact.

I have to tell you, first, that the medical student turned out to be strangely and unaccountably right in assuming it as more than probable that Arthur Holliday would marry the young lady who had given him the water-colour drawing of the landscape. That marriage took place a little more than a year after the events occurred which I have just been relating. The young couple came to live in the neighbourhood in which I was then established in practice. I was present at the wedding, and was rather surprised to find that Arthur was singularly reserved with me, both before and after his marriage, on the subject of the young lady's prior engagement. He only referred to it once, when we were alone, merely telling me, on that occasion, that his wife had done all that honour and duty required of her in the matter, and that the engagement had been broken off with the full approval of her parents. I never heard more from him than this. For three years he and his wife lived together happily. At the expiration of that time, the symptoms of a serious illness first declared themselves in Mrs. Arthur Holliday. It turned out to be a long, lingering, hopeless malady. I attended her throughout. We had been great friends when she was well, and we became more attached to each other than ever when she was ill. I had many long and interesting conversations with her in the intervals when she suffered least. The result of one of these conversations I may briefly relate, leaving you to draw any inferences from it that you please.

The interview to which I refer, occurred shortly before her death. I called one evening, as usual, and found her alone, with a look in her eyes which told me that she had been crying. She only informed me at first, that she had been depressed in spirits; but, by little and little, she became more communicative, and confessed to me that she had been looking over some old letters, which had been addressed to her, before she had seen Arthur, by a man to whom she had been engaged to be married. I asked her how the engagement came to be broken off. She replied that it had not been broken off, but that it had died out in a very mysterious way. The person to whom she was engaged – her first love, she called him – was very poor, and there was no immediate prospect of their being married. He followed my profession, and went abroad to study. They had corresponded regularly, until the time when, as she believed, he had returned to England. From that period she heard no more of him. He was of a fretful, sensitive temperament; and she feared that she might have inadvertently done or said something that offended him. However that might be, he had never written to her again; and, after waiting a year, she had married Arthur. I asked when the first estrangement had begun, and found that the time at which she ceased to hear anything of her first lover exactly corresponded with the time at which I had been called in to my mysterious patient at The Two Robins Inn.

A fortnight after that conversation, she died. In course of time, Arthur married again. Of late years, he has lived principally in London, and I have seen little or nothing of him.

I have many years to pass over before I can approach to anything like a conclusion of this fragmentary narrative. And even when that later period is reached, the little that I have to say will not occupy your attention for more than a few minutes. Between six and seven years ago, the gentleman to whom I introduced you in this room, came to me, with good professional recommendations, to fill the position of my assistant. We met, not like strangers, but like friends – the only difference between us being, that I was very much surprised to see him, and that he did not appear to be at all surprised to see me. If he was my son or my brother, I believe he could not be fonder of me than he is; but he has never volunteered any confidences since he has been here, on the subject of his past life. I saw something that was familiar to me in his face when we first met; and yet it was also something that suggested the idea of change. I had a notion once that my patient at the Inn might be a natural son of Mr. Holliday's; I had another idea that he might also have been the man who was engaged to Arthur's first wife; and I have a third idea, still clinging to me, that Mr. Lorn is the only man in England who could really enlighten me, if he chose, on both those doubtful points. His hair is not black, now, and his eyes are dimmer than the piercing eyes that I remember, but, for all that, he is very like the nameless medical student of my young days – very like him. And, sometimes, when I come home late at night, and find him asleep, and wake him, he looks, in coming to, wonderfully like the stranger at Doncaster, as he raised himself in the bed on that memorable night!

The Doctor paused. Mr. Goodchild, who had been following every word that fell from his lips up to this time, leaned forward eagerly to ask a question. Before he could say a word, the latch of the door was raised, without any warning sound of footsteps in the passage outside. A long, white, bony hand appeared through the opening, gently pushing the door, which was prevented from working freely on its hinges by a fold in the carpet under it.

'That hand! Look at that hand, Doctor!' said Mr. Goodchild, touching him.

At the same moment, the Doctor looked at Mr. Goodchild, and whispered to him, significantly:

'Hush! he has come back.'

CHAPTER III

The Cumberland Doctor's mention of Doncaster Races, inspired Mr. Francis Goodchild with the idea of going down to Doncaster to see the races. Doncaster being a good way off, and quite out of the way of the Idle Apprentices (if anything could be out of their way, who had no way), it necessarily followed that Francis perceived Doncaster in the race-week to be, of all possible idleness, the particular idleness that would completely satisfy him.

Thomas, with an enforced idleness grafted on the natural and voluntary power of his disposition, was not of this mind; objecting that a man compelled to lie on his back on a floor, a sofa, a table, a line of chairs, or anything he could get to lie upon, was not in racing condition, and that he desired nothing better than to lie where he was, enjoying himself in looking at the flies on the ceiling. But, Francis Goodchild, who had been walking round his companion in a circuit of twelve miles for two days, and had begun to doubt whether it was reserved for him ever to be idle in his life, not only overpowered this objection, but even converted Thomas Idle to a scheme he formed (another idle inspiration), of conveying the said Thomas to the seacoast, and putting his injured leg under a stream of saltwater.

Plunging into this happy conception headfore-most, Mr. Goodchild immediately referred to the county-map, and ardently discovered that the most delicious piece of seacoast to be found within the limits of England, Ireland, Scotland, Wales, the Isle of Man, and the Channel Islands, all summed up together, was Allonby on the coast of Cumberland. There was the coast of Scotland opposite to Allonby, said Mr. Goodchild with enthusiasm; there was a fine Scottish mountain on that Scottish coast; there were Scottish lights to be seen shining across the glorious Channel, and at Allonby itself there was every idle luxury (no doubt) that a water-ing-place could offer to the heart of idle man. Moreover, said Mr. Goodchild, with his finger on the map, this exquisite retreat was ap-proached by a coach-road, from a railway-station called Aspatria – a name, in a manner, suggestive of the departed glories of Greece, associated with one of the most engaging and most famous of Greek women. On this point, Mr. Goodchild continued at intervals to breathe a vein of classic fancy and eloquence exceeding-ly irksome to Mr. Idle, until it appeared that the honest English pronunciation of that Cum-berland country shortened Aspatria into 'Spat-ter.' After this supplementary discovery, Mr. Goodchild said no more about it.

By way of Spatter, the crippled Idle was car-ried, hoisted, pushed, poked, and packed, into and out of carriages, into and out of beds, into and out of tavern resting-places, until he was brought at length within sniff of the sea. And now, behold the apprentices gallantly riding into Allonby in a one-horse fly, bent upon staying in that peaceful marine valley until the turbulent Doncaster time shall come round upon the wheel, in its turn among what are in sporting registers called the 'Fixtures' for the month.

'Do you see Allonby!' asked Thomas Idle.

'I don't see it yet,' said Francis, looking out of window.

'It must be there,' said Thomas Idle.

'I don't see it,' returned Francis.

'It must be there,' repeated Thomas Idle, fretfully.

'Lord bless me!' exclaimed Francis, drawing in his head, 'I suppose this is it!'

'A watering-place,' retorted Thomas Idle, with the pardonable sharpness of an invalid, 'can't be five gentlemen in straw hats, on a form on one side of a door, and four ladies in hats and falls, on a form on another side of a door, and three geese in a dirty little brook before them, and a boy's legs hanging over a bridge (with a boy's body I suppose on the other side of the parapet), and a donkey running away. What are you talking about?

'Allonby, gentlemen,' said the most comfort-able of landladies as she opened one door of the carriage; 'Allonby, gentlemen,' said the most attentive of landlords, as he opened the other.

Thomas Idle yielded his arm to the ready Goodchild, and descended from the vehicle. Thomas, now just able to grope his way along, in a doubled-up condition, with the aid of two thick sticks, was no bad embodiment of Com-modore Trunnion, or of one of those many gallant Admirals of the stage, who have all ample fortunes, gout, thick sticks, tempers, wards, and nephews. With this distinguished naval appearance upon him, Thomas made a crablike progress up a clean little bulk-headed staircase, into a clean little bulk-headed room, where he slowly deposited himself on a sofa, with a stick on either hand of him, looking exceedingly grim.

'Francis,' said Thomas Idle, 'what do you think of this place?'

'I think,' returned Mr. Goodchild, in a glowing way, 'it is everything we expected.'

'Hah!' said Thomas Idle.

'There is the sea,' cried Mr. Goodchild, pointing out of window; 'and here,' pointing to the lunch on the table, 'are shrimps. Let us–' here Mr. Goodchild looked out of window, as if in search of something, and looked in again,–'let us eat 'em.'

The shrimps eaten and the dinner ordered, Mr. Goodchild went out to survey the watering-place. As Chorus of the Drama, without whom Thomas could make nothing of the scenery, he by-and-by returned, to have the following report screwed out of him.

In brief, it was the most delightful place ever seen.

'But,' Thomas Idle asked, 'where is it?'

'It's what you may call generally up and down the beach, here and there,' said Mr. Goodchild, with a twist of his hand.

'Proceed,' said Thomas Idle.

It was, Mr. Goodchild went on to say, in cross-examination, what you might call a primitive place. Large? No, it was not large. Who ever expected it would be large? Shape? What a question to ask! No shape. What sort of a street? Why, no street. Shops? Yes, of course (quite indignant). How many? Who ever went into a place to count the shops? Ever so many. Six? Perhaps. A library? Why, of course (indignant again). Good collection of books? Most likely – couldn't say – had seen nothing in it but a pair of scales. Any reading-room? Of course, there was a reading-room. Where?

Where! why, over there. Where was over there? Why, THERE! Let Mr. Idle carry his eye to that bit of waste ground above high-water mark, where the rank grass and loose stones were most in a litter; and he would see a sort of long, ruinous brick loft, next door to a ruinous brick outhouse, which loft had a ladder outside, to get up by. That was the reading-room, and if Mr. Idle didn't like the idea of a weaver's shuttle throbbing under a reading-room, that was his look out. HE was not to dictate, Mr. Goodchild supposed (indignant again), to the company.

'By-the-by,' Thomas Idle observed; 'the company?'

Well! (Mr. Goodchild went on to report) very nice company. Where were they? Why, there they were. Mr. Idle could see the tops of their hats, he supposed. What? Those nine straw hats again, five gentlemen's and four ladies'? Yes, to be sure. Mr. Goodchild hoped the company were not to be expected to wear helmets, to please Mr. Idle.

Beginning to recover his temper at about this point, Mr. Goodchild voluntarily reported that if you wanted to be primitive, you could be primitive here, and that if you wanted to be idle, you could be idle here. In the course of some days, he added, that there were three fishing-boats, but no rigging, and that there were plenty of fishermen who never fished. That they got their living entirely by looking at the ocean.

What nourishment they looked out of it to support their strength, he couldn't say; but, he supposed it was some sort of Iodine. The place was full of their children, who were always upside down on the public buildings (two small bridges over the brook), and always hurting themselves or one another, so that their wailings made more continual noise in the air than could have been got in a busy place. The houses people lodged in, were nowhere in particular, and were in capital accordance with the beach; being all more or less cracked and damaged as its shells were, and all empty – as its shells were. Among them, was an edifice of destitute appearance, with a number of walleyed windows in it, looking desperately out to Scotland as if for help, which said it was a Bazaar (and it ought to know), and where you might buy anything you wanted – supposing what you wanted, was a little camp-stool or a child's wheelbarrow. The brook crawled or stopped between the houses and the sea, and the donkey was always running away, and when he got into the brook he was pelted out with stones, which never hit him, and which always hit some of the children who were upside down on the public buildings, and made their lamentations louder. This donkey was the public excitement of Allonby, and was probably supported at the public expense.

The foregoing descriptions, delivered in separate items, on separate days of adventurous discovery, Mr. Goodchild severally wound up, by looking out of window, looking in again, and saying, 'But there is the sea, and here are the shrimps – let us eat 'em.'

There were fine sunsets at Allonby when the low flat beach, with its pools of water and its dry patches, changed into long bars of silver and gold in various states of burnishing, and there were fine views – on fine days – of the Scottish coast. But, when it rained at Allonby, Allonby thrown back upon its ragged self, became a kind of place which the donkey seemed to have found out, and to have his highly sagacious reasons for wishing to bolt from. Thomas Idle observed, too, that Mr. Goodchild, with a noble show of disinterestedness, became every day more ready to walk to Maryport and back, for letters; and suspicions began to harbour in the mind of Thomas, that his friend deceived him, and that Maryport was a preferable place.

Therefore, Thomas said to Francis on a day when they had looked at the sea and eaten the shrimps, 'My mind misgives me, Goodchild, that you go to Maryport, like the boy in the storybook, to ask IT to be idle with you.'

'Judge, then,' returned Francis, adopting the style of the storybook, 'with what success. I go to a region which is a bit of waterside Bristol, with a slice of Wapping, a seasoning of Wolverhampton, and a garnish of Portsmouth, and I say, "Will YOU come and be idle with me?" And it answers, "No; for I am a great deal too vaporous, and a great deal too rusty, and a great deal too muddy, and a great deal too dirty altogether; and I have ships to load, and pitch and tar to boil, and iron to hammer, and steam to get up, and smoke to make, and stone to quarry, and fifty other disagreeable things to do, and I can't be idle with you." Then I go into jagged uphill and downhill streets, where I am in the pastrycook's shop at one moment, and next moment in savage fastnesses of moor and morass, beyond the confines of civilisation, and I say to those murky and black-dusty streets, "Will YOU come and be idle with me?" To which they reply, "No, we can't, indeed, for we haven't the spirits, and we are startled by the echo of your feet on the sharp pavement, and we have so many goods in our shop-windows which nobody wants, and we have so much to do for a limited public which never comes to us to be done for, that we are altogether out of sorts and can't enjoy ourselves with any one." So I go to the Post-office, and knock at the shutter, and I say to the postmaster, "Will YOU come and be idle with me?" To which he rejoins, "No, I really can't, for I live, as you may see, in such a very little Post-office, and pass my life behind such a very little shutter, that my hand, when I put it out, is as the hand of a giant crammed through the window of a dwarf's house at a fair, and I am a mere Post-office anchorite in a cell much too small for him, and I can't get out, and I can't get in, and I have no space to be idle in, even if I would." So, the boy,' said Mr. Goodchild, concluding the tale, 'comes back with the letters after all, and lives happy never afterwards.'

But it may, not unreasonably, be asked – while Francis Goodchild was wandering hither and thither, storing his mind with perpetual observation of men and things, and sincerely believing himself to be the laziest creature in existence all the time – how did Thomas Idle, crippled and confined to the house, contrive to get through the hours of the day?

Prone on the sofa, Thomas made no attempt to get through the hours, but passively allowed the hours to get through HIM. Where other men in his situation would have read books and improved their minds, Thomas slept and rested his body. Where other men would have pondered anxiously over their future prospects, Thomas dreamed lazily of his past life. The one solitary thing he did, which most other people would have done in his place, was to resolve on making certain alterations and improvements in his mode of existence, as soon as the effects of the misfortune that had overtaken him had all passed away. Remembering that the current of his life had hitherto oozed along in one smooth stream of laziness, occasionally troubled on the surface by a slight passing ripple of industry, his present ideas on the subject of self-reform, inclined him – not as the reader may be disposed to imagine, to project schemes for a new existence of enterprise and exertion – but, on the contrary, to resolve that he would never, if he could possibly help it, be active or industrious again, throughout the whole of his future career.

It is due to Mr. Idle to relate that his mind sauntered towards this peculiar conclusion on distinct and logically-producible grounds. After reviewing, quite at his ease, and with many needful intervals of repose, the generally-placid spectacle of his past existence, he arrived at the discovery that all the great disasters which had tried his patience and equanimity in early life, had been caused by his having allowed himself to be deluded into imitating some pernicious example of activity and industry that had been set him by others. The trials to which he here alludes were three in number, and may be thus reckoned up: First, the disaster of being an unpopular and a thrashed boy at school; secondly, the disaster of falling seriously ill; thirdly, the disaster of becoming acquainted with a great bore.

The first disaster occurred after Thomas had been an idle and a popular boy at school, for some happy years. One Christmastime, he was stimulated by the evil example of a companion, whom he had always trusted and liked, to be untrue to himself, and to try for a prize at the ensuing half-yearly examination. He did try, and he got a prize – how, he did not distinctly know at the moment, and cannot remember now. No sooner, however, had the book – Moral Hints to the Young on the Value of Time – been placed in his hands, than the first troubles of his life began. The idle boys deserted him, as a traitor to their cause. The industrious boys avoided him, as a dangerous interloper; one of their number, who had always won the prize on previous occasions, expressing just resentment at the invasion of his privileges by calling Thomas into the playground, and then and there administering to him the first sound and genuine thrashing that he had ever received in his life. Unpopular from that moment, as a beaten boy, who belonged to no side and was rejected by all parties, young Idle soon lost caste with his masters, as he had previously lost caste with his schoolfellows. He had forfeited the comfortable reputation of being the one lazy member of the youthful community whom it was quite hopeless to punish. Never again did he hear the headmaster say reproachfully to an industrious boy who had committed a fault, 'I might have expected this in Thomas Idle, but it is inexcusable, sir, in you, who know better.' Never more, after winning that fatal prize, did he escape the retributive imposition, or the avenging birch. From that time, the masters made him work, and the boys would not let him play. From that time his social position steadily declined, and his life at school became a perpetual burden to him.

So, again, with the second disaster. While Thomas was lazy, he was a model of health. His first attempt at active exertion and his first suffering from severe illness are connected together by the intimate relations of cause and effect. Shortly after leaving school, he accompanied a party of friends to a cricket-field, in his natural and appropriate character of spectator only. On the ground it was discovered that the players fell short of the required number, and facile Thomas was persuaded to assist in making up the complement. At a certain appointed time, he was roused from peaceful slumber in a dry ditch, and placed before three wickets with a bat in his hand. Opposite to him, behind three more wickets, stood one of his bosom friends, filling the situation (as he was informed) of bowler. No words can describe Mr. Idle's horror and amazement, when he saw this young man – on ordinary occasions, the meekest and mildest of human beings – suddenly contract his eyebrows, compress his lips, assume the aspect of an infuriated savage, run back a few steps, then run forward, and, without the slightest previous provocation, hurl a detestably hard ball with all his might straight at Thomas's legs. Stimulated to preternatural activity of body and sharpness of eye by the instinct of self-preservation, Mr. Idle contrived, by jumping deftly aside at the right moment, and by using his bat (ridiculously narrow as it was for the purpose) as a shield, to preserve his life and limbs from the dastardly attack that had been made on both, to leave the full force of the deadly missile to strike his wicket instead of his leg; and to end the innings, so far as his side was concerned, by being immediately bowled out. Grateful for his escape, he was about to return to the dry ditch, when he was peremptorily stopped, and told that the other side was 'going in,' and that he was expected to 'field.' His conception of the whole art and mystery of 'fielding,' may be summed up in the three words of serious advice which he privately administered to himself on that trying occasion – avoid the ball. Fortified by this sound and salutary principle, he took his own course, impervious alike to ridicule and abuse. Whenever the ball came near him, he thought of his shins, and got out of the way immediately. 'Catch it!' 'Stop it!' 'Pitch it up!' were cries that passed by him like the idle wind that he regarded not. He ducked under it, he jumped over it, he whisked himself away from it on either side. Never once, through the whole innings did he and the ball come together on anything approaching to intimate terms. The unnatural activity of body which was necessarily called forth for the accomplishment of this result threw Thomas Idle, for the first time in his life, into a perspiration. The perspiration, in consequence of his want of practice in the management of that particular result of bodily activity, was suddenly checked; the inevitable chill succeeded; and that, in its turn, was followed by a fever. For the first time since his birth, Mr. Idle found himself confined to his bed for many weeks together, wasted and worn by a long illness, of which his own disastrous muscular exertion had been the sole first cause.

The third occasion on which Thomas found reason to reproach himself bitterly for the mistake of having attempted to be industrious, was connected with his choice of a calling in life. Having no interest in the Church, he appropriately selected the next best profession for a lazy man in England – the Bar. Although the Benchers of the Inns of Court have lately abandoned their good old principles, and oblige their students to make some show of studying, in Mr. Idle's time no such innovation as this existed. Young men who aspired to the honourable title of barrister were, very properly, not asked to learn anything of the law, but were merely required to eat a certain number of dinners at the table of their Hall, and to pay a certain sum of money; and were called to the Bar as soon as they could prove that they had sufficiently complied with these extremely sensible regulations. Never did Thomas move more harmoniously in concert with his elders and betters than when he was qualifying himself for admission among the barristers of his native country. Never did he feel more deeply what real laziness was in all the serene majesty of its nature, than on the memorable day when he was called to the Bar, after having carefully abstained from opening his law-books during his period of probation, except to fall asleep over them. How he could ever again have become industrious, even for the shortest period, after that great reward conferred upon his idleness, quite passes his comprehension. The kind Benchers did everything they could to show him the folly of exerting himself. They wrote out his probationary exercise for him, and never expected him even to take the trouble of reading it through when it was written. They invited him, with seven other choice spirits as lazy as himself, to come and be called to the Bar, while they were sitting over their wine and fruit after dinner. They put his oaths of allegiance, and his dreadful official denunciations of the Pope and the Pretender, so gently into his mouth, that he hardly knew how the words got there. They wheeled all their chairs softly round from the table, and sat surveying the young barristers with their backs to their bottles, rather than stand up, or adjourn to hear the exercises read. And when Mr. Idle and the seven unlabouring neophytes, ranged in order, as a class, with their backs considerately placed against a screen, had begun, in rotation, to read the exercises which they had not written, even then, each Bencher, true to the great lazy principle of the whole proceeding, stopped each neophyte before he had stammered through his first line, and bowed to him, and told him politely that he was a barrister from that moment. This was all the ceremony. It was followed by a social supper, and by the presentation, in accordance with ancient custom, of a pound of sweetmeats and a bottle of Madeira, offered in the way of needful refreshment, by each grateful neophyte to each beneficent Bencher. It may seem inconceivable that Thomas should ever have forgotten the great do-nothing principle instilled by such a ceremony as this; but it is, nevertheless, true, that certain designing students of industrious habits found him out, took advantage of his easy humour, persuaded him that it was discreditable to be a barrister and to know nothing whatever about the law, and lured him, by the force of their own evil example, into a conveyancer's chambers, to make up for lost time, and to qualify himself for practice at the Bar. After a fortnight of self-delusion, the curtain fell from his eyes; he resumed his natural character, and shut up his books. But the retribution which had hitherto always followed his little casual errors of industry followed them still. He could get away from the conveyancer's chambers, but he could not get away from one of the pupils, who had taken a fancy to him, – a tall, serious, rawboned, hardworking, disputatious pupil, with ideas of his own about reforming the Law of Real Property, who has been the scourge of Mr. Idle's existence ever since the fatal day when he fell into the mistake of attempting to study the law. Before that time his friends were all sociable idlers like himself. Since that time the burden of bearing with a hardworking young man has become part of his lot in life. Go where he will now, he can never feel certain that the rawboned pupil is not affectionately waiting for him round a corner, to tell him a little more about the Law of Real Property. Suffer as he may under the infliction, he can never complain, for he must always remember, with unavailing regret, that he has his own thoughtless industry to thank for first exposing him to the great social calamity of knowing a bore.

These events of his past life, with the significant results that they brought about, pass drowsily through Thomas Idle's memory, while he lies alone on the sofa at Allonby and elsewhere, dreaming away the time which his fellow-apprentice gets through so actively out of doors. Remembering the lesson of laziness which his past disasters teach, and bearing in mind also the fact that he is crippled in one leg because he exerted himself to go up a mountain, when he ought to have known that his proper course of conduct was to stop at the bottom of it, he holds now, and will for the future firmly continue to hold, by his new resolution never to be industrious again, on any pretence whatever, for the rest of his life. The physical results of his accident have been related in a previous chapter. The moral results now stand on record; and, with the enumeration of these, that part of the present narrative which is occupied by the Episode of The Sprained Ankle may now perhaps be considered, in all its aspects, as finished and complete.

'How do you propose that we get through this present afternoon and evening?' demanded Thomas Idle, after two or three hours of the foregoing reflections at Allonby.

Mr. Goodchild faltered, looked out of window, looked in again, and said, as he had so often said before, 'There is the sea, and here are the shrimps;– let us eat 'em'!'

But, the wise donkey was at that moment in the act of bolting: not with the irresolution of his previous efforts which had been wanting in sustained force of character, but with real vigour of purpose: shaking the dust off his mane and hind-feet at Allonby, and tearing away from it, as if he had nobly made up his mind that he never would be taken alive. At sight of this inspiring spectacle, which was visible from his sofa, Thomas Idle stretched his neck and dwelt upon it rapturously.

'Francis Goodchild,' he then said, turning to his companion with a solemn air, 'this is a delightful little Inn, excellently kept by the most comfortable of landladies and the most attentive of landlords, but – the donkey's right!'

The words, 'There is the sea, and here are the–' again trembled on the lips of Goodchild, unaccompanied however by any sound.

'Let us instantly pack the portmanteaus,' said Thomas Idle, 'pay the bill, and order a fly out, with instructions to the driver to follow the donkey!'

Mr. Goodchild, who had only wanted encouragement to disclose the real state of his feelings, and who had been pining beneath his weary secret, now burst into tears, and confessed that he thought another day in the place would be the death of him.

So, the two idle apprentices followed the donkey until the night was far advanced. Whether he was recaptured by the town-council, or is bolting at this hour through the United Kingdom, they know not. They hope he may be still bolting; if so, their best wishes are with him.

It entered Mr. Idle's head, on the borders of Cumberland, that there could be no idler place to stay at, except by snatches of a few minutes each, than a railway station. 'An intermediate station on a line – a junction – anything of that sort,' Thomas suggested. Mr. Goodchild approved of the idea as eccentric, and they journeyed on and on, until they came to such a station where there was an Inn.

'Here,' said Thomas, 'we may be luxuriously lazy; other people will travel for us, as it were, and we shall laugh at their folly.'

It was a Junction-Station, where the wooden razors before mentioned shaved the air very often, and where the sharp electric-telegraph bell was in a very restless condition. All manner of cross-lines of rails came zigzagging into it, like a Congress of iron vipers; and, a little way out of it, a pointsman in an elevated signal-box was constantly going through the motions of drawing immense quantities of beer at a public-house bar. In one direction, confused perspectives of embankments and arches were to be seen from the platform; in the other, the rails soon disentangled themselves into two tracks and shot away under a bridge, and curved round a corner. Sidings were there, in which empty luggage-vans and cattle-boxes often butted against each other as if they couldn't agree; and warehouses were there, in which great quantities of goods seemed to have taken the veil (of the consistency of tarpaulin), and to have retired from the world without any hope of getting back to it. Refreshment-rooms were there; one, for the hungry and thirsty Iron Locomotives where their coke and water were ready, and of good quality, for they were dangerous to play tricks with; the other, for the hungry and thirsty human Locomotives, who might take what they could get, and whose chief consolation was provided in the form of three terrific urns or vases of white metal, containing nothing, each forming a breastwork for a defiant and apparently much-injured woman.

Established at this Station, Mr. Thomas Idle and Mr. Francis Goodchild resolved to enjoy it. But, its contrasts were very violent, and there was also an infection in it.

First, as to its contrasts. They were only two, but they were Lethargy and Madness. The Station was either totally unconscious, or wildly raving. By day, in its unconscious state, it looked as if no life could come to it, – as if it were all rust, dust, and ashes – as if the last train for ever, had gone without issuing any Return-Tickets – as if the last Engine had uttered its last shriek and burst. One awkward shave of the air from the wooden razor, and everything changed. Tight office-doors flew open, panels yielded, books, newspapers, travelling-caps and wrappers broke out of brick walls, money chinked, conveyances oppressed by nightmares of luggage came careering into the yard, porters started up from secret places, ditto the much-injured women, the shining bell, who lived in a little tray on stilts by himself, flew into a man's hand and clamoured violently. The pointsman aloft in the signal-box made the motions of drawing, with some difficulty, hogsheads of beer. Down Train! More bear! Up Train! More beer. Cross junction Train! More beer! Cattle Train! More beer. Goods Train! Simmering, whistling, trembling, rumbling, thundering. Trains on the whole confusion of intersecting rails, crossing one another, bumping one another, hissing one another, backing to go forward, tearing into distance to come close. People frantic. Exiles seeking restoration to their native carriages, and banished to remoter climes. More beer and more bell. Then, in a minute, the Station relapsed into stupor as the stoker of the Cattle Train, the last to depart, went gliding out of it, wiping the long nose of his oilcan with a dirty pocket-handkerchief.

By night, in its unconscious state, the Station was not so much as visible. Something in the air, like an enterprising chemist's established in business on one of the boughs of Jack's beanstalk, was all that could be discerned of it under the stars. In a moment it would break out, a constellation of gas. In another moment, twenty rival chemists, on twenty rival beanstalks, came into existence. Then, the Furies would be seen, waving their lurid torches up and down the confused perspectives of embankments and arches – would be heard, too, wailing and shrieking. Then, the Station would be full of palpitating trains, as in the day; with the heightening difference that they were not so clearly seen as in the day, whereas the Station walls, starting forward under the gas, like a hippopotamus's eyes, dazzled the human locomotives with the sauce-bottle, the cheap music, the bedstead, the distorted range of buildings where the patent safes are made, the gentleman in the rain with the registered umbrella, the lady returning from the ball with the registered respirator, and all their other embellishments. And now, the human locomo-tives, creased as to their countenances and purblind as to their eyes, would swarm forth in a heap, addressing themselves to the mysterious urns and the much-injured women; while the iron locomotives, dripping fire and water, shed their steam about plentifully, making the dull oxen in their cages, with heads depressed, and foam hanging from their mouths as their red looks glanced fearfully at the surrounding terrors, seem as though they had been drinking at half-frozen waters and were hung with icicles. Through the same steam would be caught glimpses of their fellow-travellers, the sheep, getting their white kid faces together, away from the bars, and stuffing the interstices with trembling wool. Also, down among the wheels, of the man with the sledgehammer, ringing the axles of the fast night-train; against whom the oxen have a misgiving that he is the man with the pole-axe who is to come by-and-by, and so the nearest of them try to get back, and get a purchase for a thrust at him through the bars. Suddenly, the bell would ring, the steam would stop with one hiss and a yell, the chemists on the beanstalks would be busy, the avenging Furies would bestir themselves, the fast night-train would melt from eye and ear, the other trains going their ways more slowly would be heard faintly rattling in the distance like old-fashioned watches running down, the sauce-bottle and cheap music retired from view, even the bedstead went to bed, and there was no such visible thing as the Station to vex the cool wind in its blowing, or perhaps the autumn lightning, as it found out the iron rails.

The infection of the Station was this:– When it was in its raving state, the Apprentices found it impossible to be there, without labouring under the delusion that they were in a hurry. To Mr. Goodchild, whose ideas of idleness were so imperfect, this was no unpleasant hallucination, and accordingly that gentleman went through great exertions in yielding to it, and running up and down the platform, jostling everybody, under the impression that he had a highly important mission somewhere, and had not a moment to lose. But, to Thomas Idle, this contagion was so very unacceptable an incident of the situation, that he struck on the fourth day, and requested to be moved.

'This place fills me with a dreadful sensation,' said Thomas, 'of having something to do. Remove me, Francis.'

'Where would you like to go next?' was the question of the ever-engaging Goodchild.

'I have heard there is a good old Inn at Lancaster, established in a fine old house: an Inn where they give you Bride-cake every day after dinner,' said Thomas Idle. 'Let us eat Bride-cake without the trouble of being married, or of knowing anybody in that ridiculous dilemma.'

Mr. Goodchild, with a lover's sigh, assented. They departed from the Station in a violent hurry (for which, it is unnecessary to observe, there was not the least occasion), and were delivered at the fine old house at Lancaster, on the same night.

It is Mr. Goodchild's opinion, that if a visitor on his arrival at Lancaster could be accommodated with a pole which would push the opposite side of the street some yards farther off, it would be better for all parties. Protesting against being required to live in a trench, and obliged to speculate all day upon what the people can possibly be doing within a mysterious opposite window, which is a shop-window to look at, but not a shop-window in respect of its offering nothing for sale and declining to give any account whatever of itself, Mr. Goodchild concedes Lancaster to be a pleasant place. A place dropped in the midst of a charming landscape, a place with a fine ancient fragment of castle, a place of lovely walks, a place possessing staid old houses richly fitted with old Honduras mahogany, which has grown so dark with time that it seems to have got something of a retrospective mirror-quality into itself, and to show the visitor, in the depth of its grain, through all its polish, the hue of the wretched slaves who groaned long ago under old Lancaster merchants. And Mr. Goodchild adds that the stones of Lancaster do sometimes whisper, even yet, of rich men passed away – upon whose great prosperity some of these old doorways frowned sullen in the brightest weather – that their slave-gain turned to curses, as the Arabian Wizard's money turned to leaves, and that no good ever came of it, even unto the third and fourth generations, until it was wasted and gone.

It was a gallant sight to behold, the Sunday procession of the Lancaster elders to Church – all in black, and looking fearfully like a funeral without the Body – under the escort of Three Beadles.

'Think,' said Francis, as he stood at the Inn window, admiring, 'of being taken to the sacred edifice by three Beadles! I have, in my early time, been taken out of it by one Beadle; but, to be taken into it by three, O Thomas, is a distinction I shall never enjoy!'

CHAPTER IV

When Mr. Goodchild had looked out of the Lancaster Inn window for two hours on end, with great perseverance, he begun to entertain a misgiving that he was growing industrious. He therefore set himself next, to explore the country from the tops of all the steep hills in the neighbourhood.

He came back at dinnertime, red and glowing, to tell Thomas Idle what he had seen. Thomas, on his back reading, listened with great composure, and asked him whether he really had gone up those hills, and bothered himself with those views, and walked all those miles?

'Because I want to know,' added Thomas, 'what you would say of it, if you were obliged to do it?'

'It would be different, then,' said Francis. 'It would be work, then; now, it's play.'

'Play!' replied Thomas Idle, utterly repudiating the reply. 'Play! Here is a man goes systematically tearing himself to pieces, and putting himself through an incessant course of training, as if he were always under articles to fight a match for the champion's belt, and he calls it Play! Play!' exclaimed Thomas Idle, scornfully contemplating his one boot in the air. 'You CAN'T play. You don't know what it is. You make work of everything.'

The bright Goodchild amiably smiled.

'So you do,' said Thomas. 'I mean it. To me you are an absolutely terrible fellow. You do nothing like another man. Where another fellow would fall into a footbath of action or emotion, you fall into a mine. Where any other fellow would be a painted butterfly, you are a fiery dragon. Where another man would stake a sixpence, you stake your existence. If you were to go up in a balloon, you would make for Heaven; and if you were to dive into the depths of the earth, nothing short of the other place would content you. What a fellow you are, Francis!' The cheerful Goodchild laughed.

'It's all very well to laugh, but I wonder you don't feel it to be serious,' said Idle. 'A man who can do nothing by halves appears to me to be a fearful man.'

'Tom, Tom,' returned Goodchild, 'if I can do nothing by halves, and be nothing by halves, it's pretty clear that you must take me as a whole, and make the best of me.'

With this philosophical rejoinder, the airy Goodchild clapped Mr. Idle on the shoulder in a final manner, and they sat down to dinner.

'By-the-by,' said Goodchild, 'I have been over a lunatic asylum too, since I have been out.'

'He has been,' exclaimed Thomas Idle, casting up his eyes, 'over a lunatic asylum! Not content with being as great an Ass as Captain Barclay in the pedestrian way, he makes a Lunacy Commissioner of himself – for nothing!

'An immense place,' said Goodchild, 'admirable offices, very good arrangements, very good attendants; altogether a remarkable place.'

'And what did you see there?' asked Mr. Idle, adapting Hamlet's advice to the occasion, and assuming the virtue of interest, though he had it not.

'The usual thing,' said Francis Goodchild, with a sigh. 'Long groves of blighted men-and-women-trees; interminable avenues of hopeless faces; numbers, without the slightest power of really combining for any earthly purpose; a society of human creatures who have nothing in common but that they have all lost the power of being humanly social with one another.'

'Take a glass of wine with me,' said Thomas Idle, 'and let US be social.'

'In one gallery, Tom,' pursued Francis Goodchild, 'which looked to me about the length of the Long Walk at Windsor, more or less–'

'Probably less,' observed Thomas Idle.

'In one gallery, which was otherwise clear of patients (for they were all out), there was a poor little dark-chinned, meagre man, with a perplexed brow and a pensive face, stooping low over the matting on the floor, and picking out with his thumb and forefinger the course of its fibres. The afternoon sun was slanting in at the large end-window, and there were cross patches of light and shade all down the vista, made by the unseen windows and the open doors of the little sleeping-cells on either side. In about the centre of the perspective, under an arch, regardless of the pleasant weather, regardless of the solitude, regardless of approaching footsteps, was the poor little dark-chinned, meagre man, poring over the matting. "What are you doing there?" said my conductor, when we came to him. He looked up, and pointed to the matting. "I wouldn't do that, I think," said my conductor, kindly; "if I were you, I would go and read, or I would lie down if I felt tired; but I wouldn't do that." The patient considered a moment, and vacantly answered, "No, sir, I won't; I'll – I'll go and read," and so he lamely shuffled away into one of the little rooms. I turned my head before we had gone many paces. He had already come out again, and was again poring over the matting, and tracking out its fibres with his thumb and forefinger. I stopped to look at him, and it came into my mind, that probably the course of those fibres as they plaited in and out, over and under, was the only course of things in the whole wide world that it was left to him to understand – that his darkening intellect had narrowed down to the small cleft of light which showed him, "This piece was twisted this way, went in here, passed under, came out there, was carried on away here to the right where I now put my finger on it, and in this progress of events, the thing was made and came to be here." Then, I wondered whether he looked into the matting, next, to see if it could show him anything of the process through which HE came to be there, so strangely poring over it. Then, I thought how all of us, GOD help us! in our different ways are poring over our bits of matting, blindly enough, and what confusions and mysteries we make in the pattern. I had a sadder fellow-feeling with the little dark-chinned, meagre man, by that time, and I came away.'

Mr. Idle diverting the conversation to grouse, custards, and bride-cake, Mr. Goodchild followed in the same direction. The bride-cake was as bilious and indigestible as if a real Bride had cut it, and the dinner it completed was an admirable performance.

The house was a genuine old house of a very quaint description, teeming with old carvings, and beams, and panels, and having an excellent old staircase, with a gallery or upper staircase, cut off from it by a curious fence-work of old oak, or of the old Honduras Mahogany wood. It was, and is, and will be, for many a long year to come, a remarkably picturesque house; and a certain grave mystery lurking in the depth of the old mahogany panels, as if they were so many deep pools of dark water – such, indeed, as they had been much among when they were trees – gave it a very mysterious character after nightfall.

When Mr. Goodchild and Mr. Idle had first alighted at the door, and stepped into the sombre, handsome old hall, they had been received by half-a-dozen noiseless old men in black, all dressed exactly alike, who glided up the stairs with the obliging landlord and waiter – but without appearing to get into their way, or to mind whether they did or no – and who had filed off to the right and left on the old staircase, as the guests entered their sitting-room. It was then broad, bright day. But, Mr. Goodchild had said, when their door was shut, 'Who on earth are those old men?' And afterwards, both on going out and coming in, he had noticed that there were no old men to be seen.

Neither, had the old men, or any one of the old men, reappeared since. The two friends had passed a night in the house, but had seen nothing more of the old men. Mr. Goodchild, in rambling about it, had looked along passages, and glanced in at doorways, but had encountered no old men; neither did it appear that any old men were, by any member of the establishment, missed or expected.

Another odd circumstance impressed itself on their attention. It was, that the door of their sitting-room was never left untouched for a quarter of an hour. It was opened with hesitation, opened with confidence, opened a little way, opened a good way, – always clapped-to again without a word of explanation. They were reading, they were writing, they were eating, they were drinking, they were talking, they were dozing; the door was always opened at an unexpected moment, and they looked towards it, and it was clapped to again, and nobody was to be seen. When this had happened fifty times or so, Mr. Goodchild had said to his companion, jestingly: 'I begin to think, Tom, there was something wrong with those six old men.'

Night had come again, and they had been writing for two or three hours: writing, in short, a portion of the lazy notes from which these lazy sheets are taken. They had left off writing, and glasses were on the table between them. The house was closed and quiet. Around the head of Thomas Idle, as he lay upon his sofa, hovered light wreaths of fragrant smoke. The temples of Francis Goodchild, as he leaned back in his chair, with his two hands clasped behind his head, and his legs crossed, were similarly decorated.

They had been discussing several idle subjects of speculation, not omitting the strange old men, and were still so occupied, when Mr. Goodchild abruptly changed his attitude to wind up his watch. They were just becoming drowsy enough to be stopped in their talk by any such slight check. Thomas Idle, who was speaking at the moment, paused and said, 'How goes it?'

'One,' said Goodchild.

As if he had ordered One old man, and the order were promptly executed (truly, all orders were so, in that excellent hotel), the door opened, and One old man stood there.

He did not come in, but stood with the door in his hand.

'One of the six, Tom, at last!' said Mr. Good-child, in a surprised whisper.–'Sir, your plea-sure?'

'Sir, YOUR pleasure?' said the One old man.

'I didn't ring.'

'The bell did,' said the One old man.

He said BELL, in a deep, strong way, that would have expressed the church Bell.

'I had the pleasure, I believe, of seeing you, yesterday?' said Goodchild.

'I cannot undertake to say for certain,' was the grim reply of the One old man.

'I think you saw me? Did you not?'

'Saw YOU?' said the old man. 'O yes, I saw you. But, I see many who never see me.'

A chilled, slow, earthy, fixed old man. A cadaverous old man of measured speech. An old man who seemed as unable to wink, as if his eyelids had been nailed to his forehead. An old man whose eyes – two spots of fire – had no more motion than if they had been connected with the back of his skull by screws driven through it, and rivetted and bolted outside, among his grey hair.

The night had turned so cold, to Mr. Goodchild's sensations, that he shivered. He remarked lightly, and half apologetically, 'I think somebody is walking over my grave.'

'No,' said the weird old man, 'there is no one there.'

Mr. Goodchild looked at Idle, but Idle lay with his head enwreathed in smoke.

'No one there?' said Goodchild.

'There is no one at your grave, I assure you,' said the old man.

He had come in and shut the door, and he now sat down. He did not bend himself to sit, as other people do, but seemed to sink bolt upright, as if in water, until the chair stopped him.

'My friend, Mr. Idle,' said Goodchild, extremely anxious to introduce a third person into the conversation.

'I am,' said the old man, without looking at him, 'at Mr. Idle's service.'

'If you are an old inhabitant of this place,' Francis Goodchild resumed.

'Yes.'

'Perhaps you can decide a point my friend and I were in doubt upon, this morning. They hang condemned criminals at the Castle, I believe?'

'I believe so,' said the old man.

'Are their faces turned towards that noble prospect?'

'Your face is turned,' replied the old man, 'to the Castle wall. When you are tied up, you see its stones expanding and contracting violently, and a similar expansion and contraction seem to take place in your own head and breast. Then, there is a rush of fire and an earthquake, and the Castle springs into the air, and you tumble down a precipice.'

His cravat appeared to trouble him. He put his hand to his throat, and moved his neck from side to side. He was an old man of a swollen character of face, and his nose was immoveably hitched up on one side, as if by a little hook inserted in that nostril. Mr. Goodchild felt exceedingly uncomfortable, and began to think the night was hot, and not cold.

'A strong description, sir,' he observed.

A strong sensation,' the old man rejoined.

Again, Mr. Goodchild looked to Mr. Thomas Idle; but Thomas lay on his back with his face attentively turned towards the One old man, and made no sign. At this time Mr. Goodchild believed that he saw threads of fire stretch from the old man's eyes to his own, and there attach themselves. (Mr. Goodchild writes the present account of his experience, and, with the utmost solemnity, protests that he had the strongest sensation upon him of being forced to look at the old man along those two fiery films, from that moment.)

'I must tell it to you,' said the old man, with a ghastly and a stony stare.

'What?' asked Francis Goodchild.

'You know where it took place. Yonder!'

Whether he pointed to the room above, or to the room below, or to any room in that old house, or to a room in some other old house in that old town, Mr. Goodchild was not, nor is, nor ever can be, sure. He was confused by the circumstance that the right forefinger of the One old man seemed to dip itself in one of the threads of fire, light itself, and make a fiery start in the air, as it pointed somewhere. Having pointed somewhere, it went out.

'You know she was a Bride,' said the old man.

'I know they still send up Bride-cake,' Mr. Goodchild faltered. 'This is a very oppressive air.'

'She was a Bride,' said the old man. 'She was a fair, flaxen-haired, large-eyed girl, who had no character, no purpose. A weak, credulous, incapable, helpless nothing. Not like her mother. No, no. It was her father whose character she reflected.

'Her mother had taken care to secure every-thing to herself, for her own life, when the father of this girl (a child at that time) died of sheer helplessness; no other disorder – and then He renewed the acquaintance that had once subsisted between the mother and Him. He had been put aside for the flaxen-haired, large-eyed man (or nonentity) with Money.

He could overlook that for Money. He wanted compensation in Money.

'So, he returned to the side of that woman the mother, made love to her again, danced attendance on her, and submitted himself to her whims. She wreaked upon him every whim she had, or could invent. He bore it. And the more he bore, the more he wanted compensation in Money, and the more he was resolved to have it.

'But, lo! Before he got it, she cheated him. In one of her imperious states, she froze, and never thawed again. She put her hands to her head one night, uttered a cry, stiffened, lay in that attitude certain hours, and died. And he had got no compensation from her in Money, yet. Blight and Murrain on her! Not a penny.

'He had hated her throughout that second pursuit, and had longed for retaliation on her. He now counterfeited her signature to an instrument, leaving all she had to leave, to her daughter – ten years old then – to whom the property passed absolutely, and appointing himself the daughter's Guardian. When He slid it under the pillow of the bed on which she lay, He bent down in the deaf ear of Death, and whispered: "Mistress Pride, I have determined a long time that, dead or alive, you must make me compensation in Money.'

'So, now there were only two left. Which two were, He, and the fair flaxen-haired, large-eyed foolish daughter, who afterwards became the Bride.

'He put her to school. In a secret, dark, oppressive, ancient house, he put her to school with a watchful and unscrupulous woman. "My worthy lady," he said, "here is a mind to be formed; will you help me to form it? She accepted the trust. For which she, too, wanted compensation in Money, and had it.

'The girl was formed in the fear of him, and in the conviction, that there was no escape from him. She was taught, from the first, to regard him as her future husband – the man who must marry her – the destiny that overshadowed her – the appointed certainty that could never be evaded. The poor fool was soft white wax in their hands, and took the impression that they put upon her. It hardened with time. It became a part of herself. Inseparable from herself, and only to be torn away from her, by tearing life away from her.

'Eleven years she had lived in the dark house and its gloomy garden. He was jealous of the very light and air getting to her, and they kept her close. He stopped the wide chimneys, shaded the little windows, left the strong-stemmed ivy to wander where it would over the house-front, the moss to accumulate on the untrimmed fruit-trees in the red-walled garden, the weeds to over-run its green and yellow walks. He surrounded her with images of sorrow and desolation. He caused her to be filled with fears of the place and of the stories that were told of it, and then on pretext of correcting them, to be left in it in solitude, or made to shrink about it in the dark. When her mind was most depressed and fullest of terrors, then, he would come out of one of the hiding-places from which he overlooked her, and present himself as her sole resource.

'Thus, by being from her childhood the one embodiment her life presented to her of power to coerce and power to relieve, power to bind and power to loose, the ascendency over her weakness was secured. She was twenty-one years and twenty-one days old, when he brought her home to the gloomy house, his half-witted, frightened, and submissive Bride of three weeks.

'He had dismissed the governess by that time – what he had left to do, he could best do alone – and they came back, upon a rain night, to the scene of her long preparation. She turned to him upon the threshold, as the rain was dripping from the porch, and said:

'"O sir, it is the deathwatch ticking for me!"

'"Well!" he answered. "And if it were?"

'"O sir!" she returned to him, "look kindly on me, and be merciful to me! I beg your pardon.

I will do anything you wish, if you will only forgive me!"

'That had become the poor fool's constant song: "I beg your pardon," and "Forgive me!"

'She was not worth hating; he felt nothing but contempt for her. But, she had long been in the way, and he had long been weary, and the work was near its end, and had to be worked out.

'"You fool," he said. "Go up the stairs!"

'She obeyed very quickly, murmuring, "I will do anything you wish!" When he came into the Bride's Chamber, having been a little retarded by the heavy fastenings of the great door (for they were alone in the house, and he had arranged that the people who attended on them should come and go in the day), he found her withdrawn to the furthest corner, and there standing pressed against the paneling as if she would have shrunk through it: her flaxen hair all wild about her face, and her large eyes staring at him in vague terror.

'"What are you afraid of? Come and sit down by me."

'"I will do anything you wish. I beg your pardon, sir. Forgive me!" Her monotonous tune as usual.

'"Ellen, here is a writing that you must write out tomorrow, in your own hand. You may as well be seen by others, busily engaged upon it. When you have written it all fairly, and corrected all mistakes, call in any two people there may be about the house, and sign your name to it before them. Then, put it in your bosom to keep it safe, and when I sit here again tomorrow night, give it to me."

"'I will do it all, with the greatest care. I will do anything you wish."

"'Don't shake and tremble, then."

"'I will try my utmost not to do it – if you will only forgive me!"

'Next day, she sat down at her desk, and did as she had been told. He often passed in and out of the room, to observe her, and always saw her slowly and laboriously writing: repeating to herself the words she copied, in appearance quite mechanically, and without caring or endeavouring to comprehend them, so that she did her task. He saw her follow the directions she had received, in all particulars; and at night, when they were alone again in the same Bride's Chamber, and he drew his chair to the hearth, she timidly approached him from her distant seat, took the paper from her bosom, and gave it into his hand.

'It secured all her possessions to him, in the event of her death. He put her before him, face to face, that he might look at her steadily; and he asked her, in so many plain words, neither fewer nor more, did she know that?

'There were spots of ink upon the bosom of her white dress, and they made her face look whiter and her eyes look larger as she nodded her head. There were spots of ink upon the hand with which she stood before him, nervously plaiting and folding her white skirts.

'He took her by the arm, and looked her, yet more closely and steadily, in the face. "Now, die! I have done with you."

'She shrunk, and uttered a low, suppressed cry.

'"I am not going to kill you. I will not endanger my life for yours. Die!"

'He sat before her in the gloomy Bride's Chamber, day after day, night after night, looking the word at her when he did not utter it. As often as her large unmeaning eyes were raised from the hands in which she rocked her head, to the stern figure, sitting with crossed arms and knitted forehead, in the chair, they read in it, "Die!" When she dropped asleep in exhaustion, she was called back to shuddering consciousness, by the whisper, "Die!" When she fell upon her old entreaty to be pardoned, she was answered "Die!" When she had out-watched and out-suffered the long night, and the rising sun flamed into the sombre room, she heard it hailed with, "Another day and not dead?– Die!"

'Shut up in the deserted mansion, aloof from all mankind, and engaged alone in such a struggle without any respite, it came to this – that either he must die, or she. He knew it very well, and concentrated his strength against her feebleness. Hours upon hours he held her by the arm when her arm was black where he held it, and bade her Die!

'It was done, upon a windy morning, before sunrise. He computed the time to be half-past four; but, his forgotten watch had run down, and he could not be sure. She had broken away from him in the night, with loud and sudden cries – the first of that kind to which she had given vent – and he had had to put his hands over her mouth. Since then, she had been quiet in the corner of the paneling where she had sunk down; and he had left her, and had gone back with his folded arms and his knitted forehead to his chair.

'Paler in the pale light, more colourless than ever in the leaden dawn, he saw her coming, trailing herself along the floor towards him – a white wreck of hair, and dress, and wild eyes, pushing itself on by an irresolute and bending hand.

'"O, forgive me! I will do anything. O, sir, pray tell me I may live!"

'"Die!"

'"Are you so resolved? Is there no hope for me?"

'"Die!"

'Her large eyes strained themselves with wonder and fear; wonder and fear changed to reproach; reproach to blank nothing. It was done. He was not at first so sure it was done, but that the morning sun was hanging jewels in her hair – he saw the diamond, emerald, and ruby, glittering among it in little points, as he stood looking down at her – when he lifted her and laid her on her bed.

'She was soon laid in the ground. And now they were all gone, and he had compensated himself well.

'He had a mind to travel. Not that he meant to waste his Money, for he was a pinching man and liked his Money dearly (liked nothing else, indeed), but, that he had grown tired of the desolate house and wished to turn his back upon it and have done with it. But, the house was worth Money, and Money must not be thrown away. He determined to sell it before he went. That it might look the less wretched and bring a better price, he hired some labourers to work in the overgrown garden; to cut out the dead wood, trim the ivy that drooped in heavy masses over the windows and gables, and clear the walks in which the weeds were growing mid-leg high.

'He worked, himself, along with them. He worked later than they did, and, one evening at dusk, was left working alone, with his billhook in his hand. One autumn evening, when the Bride was five weeks dead.

'"It grows too dark to work longer," he said to himself, "I must give over for the night."

'He detested the house, and was loath to enter it. He looked at the dark porch waiting for him like a tomb, and felt that it was an accursed house. Near to the porch, and near to where he stood, was a tree whose branches waved before the old bay-window of the Bride's Chamber, where it had been done. The tree swung suddenly, and made him start. It swung again, although the night was still. Looking up into it, he saw a figure among the branches.

'It was the figure of a young man. The face looked down, as his looked up; the branches cracked and swayed; the figure rapidly descended, and slid upon its feet before him. A slender youth of about her age, with long light brown hair.

'"What thief are you?" he said, seizing the youth by the collar.

'The young man, in shaking himself free, swung him a blow with his arm across the face and throat. They closed, but the young man got from him and stepped back, crying, with great eagerness and horror, "Don't touch me! I would as lieve be touched by the Devil!"

'He stood still, with his billhook in his hand, looking at the young man. For, the young man's look was the counterpart of her last look, and he had not expected ever to see that again.

"'I am no thief. Even if I were, I would not have a coin of your wealth, if it would buy me the Indies. You murderer!"

"'What!"

"'I climbed it," said the young man, pointing up into the tree, "for the first time, nigh four years ago. I climbed it, to look at her. I saw her. I spoke to her. I have climbed it, many a time, to watch and listen for her. I was a boy, hidden among its leaves, when from that bay-window she gave me this!"

'He showed a tress of flaxen hair, tied with a mourning ribbon.

"'Her life," said the young man, "was a life of mourning. She gave me this, as a token of it, and a sign that she was dead to every one but you. If I had been older, if I had seen her sooner, I might have saved her from you. But, she was fast in the web when I first climbed the tree, and what could I do then to break it!"

'In saying those words, he burst into a fit of sobbing and crying: weakly at first, then passion- ately.

'"Murderer! I climbed the tree on the night when you brought her back. I heard her, from the tree, speak of the deathwatch at the door. I was three times in the tree while you were shut up with her, slowly killing her. I saw her, from the tree, lie dead upon her bed. I have watched you, from the tree, for proofs and traces of your guilt. The manner of it, is a mystery to me yet, but I will pursue you until you have rendered up your life to the hangman. You shall never, until then, be rid of me. I loved her! I can know no relenting towards you. Murderer, I loved her!"

'The youth was bareheaded, his hat having flut- tered away in his descent from the tree. He moved towards the gate. He had to pass – Him – to get to it. There was breadth for two old-fashioned carriages abreast; and the youth's abhorrence, openly expressed in every feature of his face and limb of his body, and very hard to bear, had verge enough to keep itself at a distance in. He (by which I mean the other) had not stirred hand or foot, since he had stood still to look at the boy. He faced round, now, to fol- low him with his eyes. As the back of the bare light-brown head was turned to him, he saw a red curve stretch from his hand to it. He knew, before he threw the billhook, where it had alighted – I say, had alighted, and not, would alight; for, to his clear perception the thing was done before he did it. It cleft the head, and it remained there, and the boy lay on his face.

'He buried the body in the night, at the foot of the tree. As soon as it was light in the morning, he worked at turning up all the ground near the tree, and hacking and hewing at the neighbouring bushes and undergrowth. When the labourers came, there was nothing suspicious, and nothing suspected.

'But, he had, in a moment, defeated all his precautions, and destroyed the triumph of the scheme he had so long concerted, and so successfully worked out. He had got rid of the Bride, and had acquired her fortune without endangering his life; but now, for a death by which he had gained nothing, he had evermore to live with a rope around his neck.

'Beyond this, he was chained to the house of gloom and horror, which he could not endure. Being afraid to sell it or to quit it, lest discovery should be made, he was forced to live in it. He hired two old people, man and wife, for his servants; and dwelt in it, and dreaded it. His great difficulty, for a long time, was the garden. Whether he should keep it trim, whether he should suffer it to fall into its former state of neglect, what would be the least likely way of attracting attention to it?

'He took the middle course of gardening, himself, in his evening leisure, and of then calling the old serving-man to help him; but, of never letting him work there alone. And he made himself an arbour over against the tree, where he could sit and see that it was safe.

'As the seasons changed, and the tree changed, his mind perceived dangers that were always changing. In the leafy time, he perceived that the upper boughs were growing into the form of the young man – that they made the shape of him exactly, sitting in a forked branch swinging in the wind. In the time of the falling leaves, he perceived that they came down from the tree, forming telltale letters on the path, or that they had a tendency to heap themselves into a churchyard mound above the grave. In the winter, when the tree was bare, he perceived that the boughs swung at him the ghost of the blow the young man had given, and that they threatened him openly. In the spring, when the sap was mounting in the trunk, he asked himself, were the dried-up particles of blood mounting with it: to make out more obviously this year than last, the leaf-screened figure of the young man, swinging in the wind?

'However, he turned his Money over and over, and still over. He was in the dark trade, the gold-dust trade, and most secret trades that yielded great returns. In ten years, he had turned his Money over, so many times, that the traders and shippers who had dealings with him, absolutely did not lie – for once – when they declared that he had increased his fortune, Twelve Hundred Per Cent.

'He possessed his riches one hundred years ago, when people could be lost easily. He had heard who the youth was, from hearing of the search that was made after him; but, it died away, and the youth was forgotten.

'The annual round of changes in the tree had been repeated ten times since the night of the burial at its foot, when there was a great thunderstorm over this place. It broke at midnight, and roared until morning. The first intelligence he heard from his old serving-man that morning, was, that the tree had been struck by Lightning.

'It had been riven down the stem, in a very surprising manner, and the stem lay in two blighted shafts: one resting against the house, and one against a portion of the old red garden-wall in which its fall had made a gap. The fissure went down the tree to a little above the earth, and there stopped. There was great curiosity to see the tree, and, with most of his former fears revived, he sat in his arbour – grown quite an old man – watching the people who came to see it.

'They quickly began to come, in such dangerous numbers, that he closed his garden-gate and refused to admit any more. But, there were certain men of science who travelled from a distance to examine the tree, and, in an evil hour, he let them in!– Blight and Murrain on them, let them in!

'They wanted to dig up the ruin by the roots, and closely examine it, and the earth about it. Never, while he lived! They offered money for it. They! Men of science, whom he could have bought by the gross, with a scratch of his pen! He showed them the garden-gate again, and locked and barred it.

'But they were bent on doing what they wanted to do, and they bribed the old serving-man – a thankless wretch who regularly complained when he received his wages, of being underpaid – and they stole into the garden by night with their lanterns, picks, and shovels, and fell to at the tree. He was lying in a turret-room on the other side of the house (the Bride's Chamber had been unoccupied ever since), but he soon dreamed of picks and shovels, and got up.

'He came to an upper window on that side, whence he could see their lanterns, and them, and the loose earth in a heap which he had himself disturbed and put back, when it was last turned to the air. It was found! They had that minute lighted on it. They were all bending over it. One of them said, "The skull is fractured;" and another, "See here the bones;" and another, "See here the clothes;" and then the first struck in again, and said, "A rusty billhook!"

'He became sensible, next day, that he was already put under a strict watch, and that he could go nowhere without being followed. Before a week was out, he was taken and laid in hold. The circumstances were gradually pieced together against him, with a desperate malignity, and an appalling ingenuity. But, see the justice of men, and how it was extended to him! He was further accused of having poisoned that girl in the Bride's Chamber. He, who had carefully and expressly avoided imperilling a hair of his head for her, and who had seen her die of her own incapacity!

'There was doubt for which of the two murders he should be first tried; but, the real one was chosen, and he was found Guilty, and cast for death. Bloodthirsty wretches! They would have made him Guilty of anything, so set they were upon having his life.

'His money could do nothing to save him, and he was hanged. I am He, and I was hanged at Lancaster Castle with my face to the wall, a hundred years ago!'

At this terrific announcement, Mr. Goodchild tried to rise and cry out. But, the two fiery lines extending from the old man's eyes to his own, kept him down, and he could not utter a sound. His sense of hearing, however, was acute, and he could hear the clock strike Two. No sooner had he heard the clock strike Two, than he saw before him Two old men!

TWO.

The eyes of each, connected with his eyes by two films of fire: each, exactly like the other: each, addressing him at precisely one and the same instant: each, gnashing the same teeth in the same head, with the same twitched nostril above them, and the same suffused expression around it. Two old men. Differing in nothing, equally distinct to the sight, the copy no fainter than the original, the second as real as the first.

'At what time,' said the Two old men, 'did you arrive at the door below?'

'At Six.'

'And there were Six old men upon the stairs!'

Mr. Goodchild having wiped the perspiration from his brow, or tried to do it, the Two old men proceeded in one voice, and in the singular number:

'I had been anatomised, but had not yet had my skeleton put together and re-hung on an iron hook, when it began to be whispered that the Bride's Chamber was haunted. It WAS haunted, and I was there.

'WE were there. She and I were there. I, in the chair upon the hearth; she, a white wreck again, trailing itself towards me on the floor. But, I was the speaker no more, and the one word that she said to me from midnight until dawn was, 'Live!'

'The youth was there, likewise. In the tree outside the window. Coming and going in the moonlight, as the tree bent and gave. He has, ever since, been there, peeping in at me in my torment; revealing to me by snatches, in the pale lights and slatey shadows where he comes and goes, bareheaded – a billhook, standing edgewise in his hair.

'In the Bride's Chamber, every night from midnight until dawn – one month in the year excepted, as I am going to tell you – he hides in the tree, and she comes towards me on the floor; always approaching; never coming nearer; always visible as if by moonlight, whether the moon shines or no; always saying, from midnight until dawn, her one word, "Live!"'

'But, in the month wherein I was forced out of this life – this present month of thirty days – the Bride's Chamber is empty and quiet. Not so my old dungeon. Not so the rooms where I was restless and afraid, ten years. Both are fitfully haunted then. At One in the morning. I am what you saw me when the clock struck that hour – One old man. At Two in the morning, I am Two old men. At Three, I am Three. By Twelve at noon, I am Twelve old men, One for every hundred per cent. of old gain. Every one of the Twelve, with Twelve times my old power of suffering and agony. From that hour until Twelve at night, I, Twelve old men in anguish and fearful foreboding, wait for the coming of the executioner. At Twelve at night, I, Twelve old men turned off, swing invisible outside Lancaster Castle, with Twelve faces to the wall!

'When the Bride's Chamber was first haunted, it was known to me that this punishment would never cease, until I could make its nature, and my story, known to two living men together. I waited for the coming of two living men together into the Bride's Chamber, years upon years. It was infused into my knowledge (of the means I am ignorant) that if two living men, with their eyes open, could be in the Bride's Chamber at One in the morning, they would see me sitting in my chair.

'At length, the whispers that the room was spiritually troubled, brought two men to try the adventure. I was scarcely struck upon the hearth at midnight (I come there as if the Lightning blasted me into being), when I heard them ascending the stairs. Next, I saw them enter. One of them was a bold, gay, active man, in the prime of life, some five and forty years of age; the other, a dozen years younger. They brought provisions with them in a basket, and bottles. A young woman accompanied them, with wood and coals for the lighting of the fire. When she had lighted it, the bold, gay, active man accompanied her along the gallery outside the room, to see her safely down the staircase, and came back laughing.

'He locked the door, examined the chamber, put out the contents of the basket on the table before the fire – little recking of me, in my appointed station on the hearth, close to him – and filled the glasses, and ate and drank. His companion did the same, and was as cheerful and confident as he: though he was the leader. When they had supped, they laid pistols on the table, turned to the fire, and began to smoke their pipes of foreign make.

'They had travelled together, and had been much together, and had an abundance of subjects in common. In the midst of their talking and laughing, the younger man made a reference to the leader's being always ready for any adventure; that one, or any other. He replied in these words:

'"Not quite so, Dick; if I am afraid of nothing else, I am afraid of myself."

'His companion seeming to grow a little dull, asked him, in what sense? How?

'"Why, thus," he returned. "Here is a Ghost to be disproved. Well! I cannot answer for what my fancy might do if I were alone here, or what tricks my senses might play with me if they had me to themselves. But, in company with another man, and especially with Dick, I would consent to outface all the Ghosts that were ever of in the universe."

"'I had not the vanity to suppose that I was of so much importance tonight," said the other.

"'Of so much," rejoined the leader, more seriously than he had spoken yet, "that I would, for the reason I have given, on no account have undertaken to pass the night here alone."

'It was within a few minutes of One. The head of the younger man had drooped when he made his last remark, and it drooped lower now.

"'Keep awake, Dick!" said the leader, gaily. "The small hours are the worst."

'He tried, but his head drooped again.

"'Dick!" urged the leader. "Keep awake!"

"'I can't," he indistinctly muttered. "I don't know what strange influence is stealing over me. I can't."

'His companion looked at him with a sudden horror, and I, in my different way, felt a new horror also; for, it was on the stroke of One, and I felt that the second watcher was yielding to me, and that the curse was upon me that I must send him to sleep.

'"Get up and walk, Dick!" cried the leader. "Try!"

'It was in vain to go behind the slumber's chair and shake him. One o'clock sounded, and I was present to the elder man, and he stood transfixed before me.

'To him alone, I was obliged to relate my story, without hope of benefit. To him alone, I was an awful phantom making a quite useless confession. I foresee it will ever be the same. The two living men together will never come to release me. When I appear, the senses of one of the two will be locked in sleep; he will neither see nor hear me; my communication will ever be made to a solitary listener, and will ever be unserviceable. Woe! Woe! Woe!'

As the Two old men, with these words, wrung their hands, it shot into Mr. Goodchild's mind that he was in the terrible situation of being virtually alone with the spectre, and that Mr. Idle's immoveability was explained by his having been charmed asleep at One o'clock. In the terror of this sudden discovery which produced an indescribable dread, he struggled so hard to get free from the four fiery threads, that he snapped them, after he had pulled them out to a great width. Being then out of bonds, he caught up Mr. Idle from the sofa and rushed downstairs with him.

'What are you about, Francis?' demanded Mr. Idle. 'My bedroom is not down here. What the deuce are you carrying me at all for? I can walk with a stick now. I don't want to be carried. Put me down.'

Mr. Goodchild put him down in the old hall, and looked about him wildly.

'What are you doing? Idiotically plunging at your own sex, and rescuing them or perishing in the attempt?' asked Mr. Idle, in a highly petulant state.

'The One old man!' cried Mr. Goodchild, distract-edly,–'and the Two old men!'

Mr. Idle deigned no other reply than 'The One old woman, I think you mean,' as he began hobbling his way back up the staircase, with the assistance of its broad balustrade.

'I assure you, Tom,' began Mr. Goodchild, attending at his side, 'that since you fell asleep–'

'Come, I like that!' said Thomas Idle, 'I haven't closed an eye!'

With the peculiar sensitiveness on the subject of the disgraceful action of going to sleep out of bed, which is the lot of all mankind, Mr. Idle persisted in this declaration. The same peculiar sensitiveness impelled Mr. Goodchild, on being taxed with the same crime, to repudiate it with honourable resentment. The settlement of the question of The One old man and The Two old men was thus presently complicated, and soon made quite impracticable. Mr. Idle said it was all Bride-cake, and fragments, newly arranged, of things seen and thought about in the day. Mr. Goodchild said how could that be, when he hadn't been asleep, and what right could Mr. Idle have to say so, who had been asleep? Mr. Idle said he had never been asleep, and never did go to sleep, and that Mr. Goodchild, as a general rule, was always asleep. They consequently parted for the rest of the night, at their bedroom doors, a little ruffled. Mr. Goodchild's last words were, that he had had, in that real and tangible old sitting-room of that real and tangible old Inn (he supposed Mr. Idle denied its existence?), every sensation and experience, the present record of which is now within a line or two of completion; and that he would write it out and print it every word. Mr. Idle returned that he might if he liked – and he did like, and has now done it.

CHAPTER V

Two of the many passengers by a certain late Sunday evening train, Mr. Thomas Idle and Mr. Francis Goodchild, yielded up their tickets at a little rotten platform (converted into artificial touchwood by smoke and ashes), deep in the manufacturing bosom of Yorkshire. A mysterious bosom it appeared, upon a damp, dark, Sunday night, dashed through in the train to the music of the whirling wheels, the panting of the engine, and the part-singing of hundreds of third-class excursionists, whose vocal efforts 'bobbed arayound' from sacred to profane, from hymns, to our transatlantic sisters the Yankee Gal and Mairy Anne, in a remarkable way. There seemed to have been some large vocal gathering near to every lonely station on the line. No town was visible, no village was visible, no light was visible; but, a multitude got out singing, and a multitude got in singing, and the second multitude took up the hymns, and adopted our transatlantic sisters, and sang of their own egregious wickedness, and of their bobbing arayound, and of how the ship it was ready and the wind it was fair, and they were bayound for the sea, Mairy Anne, until they in their turn became a getting-out multitude, and were replaced by another getting-in multitude, who did the same. And at every station, the getting-in multitude, with an artistic reference to the completeness of their chorus, incessantly cried, as with one voice while scuffling into the carriages, 'We mun aa' gang toogither!'

The singing and the multitudes had trailed off as the lonely places were left and the great towns were neared, and the way had lain as silently as a train's way ever can, over the vague black streets of the great gulfs of towns, and among their branchless woods of vague black chimneys. These towns looked, in the cinderous wet, as though they had one and all been on fire and were just put out – a dreary and quenched panorama, many miles long.

Thus, Thomas and Francis got to Leeds; of which enterprising and important commercial centre it may be observed with delicacy, that you must either like it very much or not at all. Next day, the first of the Race-Week, they took train to Doncaster.

And instantly the character, both of travellers and of luggage, entirely changed, and no other business than race-business any longer existed on the face of the earth. The talk was all of horses and 'John Scott.' Guards whispered behind their hands to stationmasters, of horses and John Scott. Men in cutaway coats and speckled cravats fastened with peculiar pins, and with the large bones of their legs developed under tight trousers, so that they should look as much as possible like horses' legs, paced up and down by twos at junction-stations, speaking low and moodily of horses and John Scott. The young clergyman in the black strait-waistcoat, who occupied the middle seat of the carriage, expounded in his peculiar pulpit-accent to the young and lovely Reverend Mrs. Crinoline, who occupied the opposite middle-seat, a few passages of rumour relative to 'Oartheth, my love, and Mithter John Eth-COTT.' A bandy vagabond, with a head like a Dutch cheese, in a fustian stable-suit, attending on a horsebox and going about the platforms with a halter hanging round his neck like a Calais burgher of the ancient period much degenerated, was courted by the best society, by reason of what he had to hint, when not engaged in eating straw, concerning 't'harses and Joon Scott.' The engine-driver himself, as he applied one eye to his large stationary double-eye-glass on the engine, seemed to keep the other open, sideways, upon horses and John Scott.

Breaks and barriers at Doncaster Station to keep the crowd off; temporary wooden avenues of ingress and egress, to help the crowd on. Forty extra porters sent down for this present blessed Race-Week, and all of them making up their betting-books in the lamp-room or somewhere else, and none of them to come and touch the luggage. Travellers disgorged into an open space, a howling wilderness of idle men. All work but race-work at a standstill; all men at a standstill. 'Ey my word! Deant ask noon o' us to help wi' t'luggage. Bock your opinion loike a mon. Coom! Dang it, coom, t'harses and Joon

Scott!' In the midst of the idle men, all the fly horses and omnibus horses of Doncaster and parts adjacent, rampant, rearing, backing, plunging, shying – apparently the result of their hearing of nothing but their own order and John Scott.

Grand Dramatic Company from London for the Race-Week. Poses Plastiques in the Grand Assembly Room up the Stable-Yard at seven and nine each evening, for the Race-Week. Grand Alliance Circus in the field beyond the bridge, for the Race-Week. Grand Exhibition of Aztec Lilliputians, important to all who want to be horrified cheap, for the Race-Week. Lodgings, grand and not grand, but all at grand prices, ranging from ten pounds to twenty, for the Grand Race-Week!

Rendered giddy enough by these things, Messieurs Idle and Goodchild repaired to the quarters they had secured beforehand, and Mr. Goodchild looked down from the window into the surging street.

'By Heaven, Tom!' cried he, after contemplating it, 'I am in the Lunatic Asylum again, and these are all mad people under the charge of a body of designing keepers!'

All through the Race-Week, Mr. Goodchild never divested himself of this idea. Every day he looked out of window, with something of the dread of Lemuel Gulliver looking down at men after he returned home from the horse-country; and every day he saw the Lunatics, horse-mad, betting-mad, drunken-mad, vice-mad, and the designing Keepers always after them. The idea pervaded, like the second colour in shot-silk, the whole of Mr. Goodchild's impressions. They were much as follows:

Monday, midday. Races not to begin until tomorrow, but all the mob-Lunatics out, crowding the pavements of the one main street of pretty and pleasant Doncaster, crowding the road, particularly crowding the outside of the Betting Rooms, whooping and shouting loudly after all passing vehicles. Frightened lunatic horses occasionally running away, with infinite clatter. All degrees of men, from peers to paupers, betting incessantly. Keepers very watchful, and taking all good chances. An awful family likeness among the Keepers, to Mr. Palmer and Mr. Thurtell. With some knowledge of expression and some acquaintance with heads (thus writes Mr. Goodchild), I never have seen anywhere, so many repetitions of one class of countenance and one character of head (both evil) as in this street at this time. Cunning, covetousness, secrecy, cold calculation, hard callousness and dire insensibility, are the uniform Keeper characteristics. Mr. Palmer passes me five times in five minutes, and, so I go down the street, the back of Mr. Thurtell's skull is always going on before me.

Monday evening. Town lighted up; more Lunatics out than ever; a complete choke and stoppage of the thoroughfare outside the Betting Rooms. Keepers, having dined, pervade the Betting Rooms, and sharply snap at the moneyed Lunatics. Some Keepers flushed with drink, and some not, but all close and calculating. A vague echoing roar of 't'harses' and 't'races' always rising in the air, until midnight, at about which period it dies away in occasional drunken songs and straggling yells. But, all night, some unmannerly drinking-house in the neighbourhood opens its mouth at intervals and spits out a man too drunk to be retained: who thereupon makes what uproarious protest may be left in him, and either falls asleep where he tumbles, or is carried off in custody.

Tuesday morning, at daybreak. A sudden rising, as it were out of the earth, of all the obscene creatures, who sell 'correct cards of the races.' They may have been coiled in corners, or sleeping on doorsteps, and, having all passed the night under the same set of circumstances, may all want to circulate their blood at the same time; but, however that may be, they spring into existence all at once and together, as though a new Cadmus had sown a racehorse's teeth. There is nobody up, to buy the cards; but, the cards are madly cried. There is no patronage to quarrel for; but, they madly quarrel and fight. Conspicuous among these hyaenas, as breakfast-time discloses, is a fearful creature in the general semblance of a man: shaken off his next-to-no legs by drink and devilry, bareheaded and barefooted, with a great shock of hair like a horrible broom, and nothing on him but a ragged pair of trousers and a pink glazed-calico coat – made on him – so very tight that it is as evident that he could never take it off, as that he never does. This hideous apparition, inconceivably drunk, has a terrible power of making a gonglike imitation of the braying of an ass: which feat requires that he should lay his right jaw in his begrimed right paw, double himself up, and shake his bray out of himself, with much staggering on his next-to-no legs, and much twirling of his horrible broom, as if it were a mop. From the present minute, when he comes in sight holding up his cards to the windows, and hoarsely proposing purchase to My Lord, Your Excellency, Colonel, the Noble Captain, and Your Honourable Worship – from the present minute until the Grand Race-Week is finished, at all hours of the morning, evening, day, and night, shall the town reverberate, at capricious intervals, to the brays of this frightful animal the Gong-donkey.

No very great racing today, so no very great amount of vehicles: though there is a good sprinkling, too: from farmers' carts and gigs, to carriages with post-horses and to fours-in-hand, mostly coming by the road from York, and passing on straight through the main street to the Course. A walk in the wrong direction may be a better thing for Mr. Goodchild today than the Course, so he walks in the wrong direction. Everybody gone to the races. Only children in the street. Grand Alliance Circus deserted; not one Star-Rider left; omnibus which forms the Pay-Place, having on separate panels Pay here for the Boxes, Pay here for the Pit, Pay here for the Gallery, hove down in a corner and locked up; nobody near the tent but the man on his knees on the grass, who is making the paper balloons for the Star young gentlemen to jump through tonight. A pleasant road, pleasantly wooded. No labourers working in the fields; all gone 't'races.' The few late wenders of their way 't'races,' who are yet left driving on the road, stare in amazement at the recluse who is not going 't'races.' Roadside innkeeper has gone 't'races.' Turnpike-man has gone 't'races.' His thrifty wife, washing clothes at the tollhouse door, is going 't'races' tomorrow. Perhaps there may be no one left to take the toll tomorrow; who knows? Though assuredly that would be neither turnpike-like nor Yorkshire-like. The very wind and dust seem to be hurrying 't'races,' as they briskly pass the only wayfarer on the road. In the distance, the Railway Engine, waiting at the town-end, shrieks despairingly. Nothing but the difficulty of getting off the Line, restrains that Engine from going 't'races,' too, it is very clear.

At night, more Lunatics out than last night – and more Keepers. The latter very active at the Betting Rooms, the street in front of which is now impassable. Mr. Palmer as before. Mr. Thurtell as before. Roar and uproar as before. Gradual subsidence as before. Unmannerly drinking-house expectorates as before. Drunken negro-melodists, Gong-donkey, and correct cards, in the night.

On Wednesday morning, the morning of the great St. Leger, it becomes apparent that there has been a great influx since yesterday, both of Lunatics and Keepers. The families of the tradesmen over the way are no longer within human ken; their places know them no more; ten, fifteen, and twenty guinea-lodgers fill them. At the pastry-cook's second-floor window, a Keeper is brushing Mr. Thurtell's hair – thinking it his own. In the wax-chandler's attic, another Keeper is putting on Mr. Palmer's braces. In the gunsmith's nursery, a Lunatic is shaving himself. In the serious stationer's best sitting-room, three Lunatics are taking a combination-breakfast, praising the (cook's) devil, and drinking neat brandy in an atmosphere of last midnight's cigars. No family sanctuary is free from our Angelic messengers – we put up at the Angel – who in the guise of extra waiters for the grand Race-Week, rattle in and out of the most secret chambers of everybody's house, with dishes and tin covers, decanters, soda-water bottles, and glasses. An hour later. Down the street and up the street, as far as eyes can see and a good deal farther, there is a dense crowd; outside the Betting Rooms it is like a great struggle at a theatre door – in the days of theatres; or at the vestibule of the Spurgeon temple – in the days of Spurgeon. An hour later. Fusing into this crowd, and somehow getting through it, are all kinds of conveyances, and all kinds of foot-passengers; carts, with brick-makers and brick-makeresses jolting up and down on planks; drags, with the needful grooms behind, sitting cross-armed in the needful manner, and slanting themselves backward from the soles of their boots at the needful angle; postboys, in the shining hats and smart jackets of the olden time, when stokers were not; beautiful Yorkshire horses, gallantly driven by their own breeders and masters. Under every pole, and every shaft, and every horse, and every wheel as it would seem, the Gong-donkey – metallically braying, when not struggling for life, or whipped out of the way.

By one o'clock, all this stir has gone out of the streets, and there is no one left in them but Francis Goodchild. Francis Goodchild will not be left in them long; for, he too is on his way, 't'races.'

A most beautiful sight, Francis Goodchild finds 't'races' to be, when he has left fair Doncaster behind him, and comes out on the free course, with its agreeable prospect, its quaint Red House oddly changing and turning as Francis turns, its green grass, and fresh heath. A free course and an easy one, where Francis can roll smoothly where he will, and can choose between the start, or the coming-in, or the turn behind the brow of the hill, or any out-of-the-way point where he lists to see the throbbing horses straining every nerve, and making the sympathetic earth throb as they come by. Francis much delights to be, not in the Grand Stand, but where he can see it, rising against the sky with its vast tiers of little white dots of faces, and its last high rows and corners of people, looking like pins stuck into an enormous pincushion – not quite so symmetrically as his orderly eye could wish, when people change or go away. When the race is nearly run out, it is as good as the race to him to see the flutter among the pins, and the change in them from dark to light, as hats are taken off and waved. Not less full of interest, the loud anticipation of the winner's name, the swelling, and the final, roar; then, the quick dropping of all the pins out of their places, the revelation of the shape of the bare pincushion, and the closing-in of the whole host of Lunatics and Keepers, in the rear of the three horses with bright-coloured riders, who have not yet quite subdued their gallop though the contest is over.

Mr. Goodchild would appear to have been by no means free from lunacy himself at 't'races,' though not of the prevalent kind. He is suspected by Mr. Idle to have fallen into a dreadful state concerning a pair of little lilac gloves and a little bonnet that he saw there. Mr. Idle asserts, that he did afterwards repeat at the Angel, with an appearance of being lunatically seized, some rhapsody to the following effect: 'O little lilac gloves! And O winning little bonnet, making in conjunction with her golden hair quite a Glory in the sunlight round the pretty head, why anything in the world but you and me! Why may not this day's running-of horses, to all the rest: of precious sands of life to me – be prolonged through an everlasting autumn-sunshine, without a sunset! Slave of the Lamp, or Ring, strike me yonder gallant equestrian Clerk of the Course, in the scarlet coat, motionless on the green grass for ages! Friendly Devil on Two Sticks, for ten times ten thousands years, keep Blink-Bonny jibbing at the post, and let us have no start! Arab drums, powerful of old to summon Genii in the desert, sound of yourselves and raise a troop for me in the desert of my heart, which shall so enchant this dusty barouche (with a conspicuous excise-plate, resembling the Collector's doorplate at a turnpike), that I, within it, loving the little lilac gloves, the winning little bonnet, and the dear unknown-wearer with the golden hair, may wait by her side for ever, to see a Great St. Leger that shall never be run!'

Thursday morning. After a tremendous night of crowding, shouting, drinking-house expectoration, Gong-donkey, and correct cards. Symptoms of yesterday's gains in the way of drink, and of yesterday's losses in the way of money, abundant. Money-losses very great. As usual, nobody seems to have won; but, large losses and many losers are unquestionable facts. Both Lunatics and Keepers, in general very low. Several of both kinds look in at the chemist's while Mr. Goodchild is making a purchase there, to be 'picked up.' One red-eyed Lunatic, flushed, faded, and disordered, enters hurriedly and cries savagely, 'Hond us a gloss of sal volatile in wather, or soom dommed thing o' thot sart!' Faces at the Betting Rooms very long, and a tendency to bite nails observable. Keepers likewise given this morning to standing about solitary, with their hands in their pockets, looking down at their boots as they fit them into cracks of the pavement, and then looking up whistling and walking away. Grand Alliance Circus out, in procession; buxom lady-member of Grand Alliance, in crimson riding-habit, fresher to look at, even in her paint under the day sky, than the cheeks of Lunatics or Keepers. Spanish Cavalier appears to have lost yesterday, and jingles his bossed bridle with disgust, as if he were paying. Reaction also apparent at the Guildhall opposite, whence certain pickpockets come out handcuffed together, with that peculiar walk which is never seen under any other circumstances – a walk expressive of going to jail, game, but still of jails being in bad taste and arbitrary, and how would YOU like it if it was you instead of me, as it ought to be! midday. Town filled as yesterday, but not so full; and emptied as yesterday, but not so empty. In the evening, Angel ordinary where every Lunatic and Keeper has his modest daily meal of turtle, venison, and wine, not so crowded as yesterday, and not so noisy. At night, the theatre. More abstracted faces in it than one ever sees at public assemblies; such faces wearing an expression which strongly reminds Mr. Goodchild of the boys at school who were 'going up next,' with their arithmetic or mathematics. These boys are, no doubt, going up tomorrow with THEIR sums and figures. Mr. Palmer and Mr. Thurtell in the boxes O. P. Mr. Thurtell and Mr. Palmer in the boxes P. S. The firm of Thurtell, Palmer, and Thurtell, in the boxes Centre. A most odious tendency observable in these distinguished gentlemen to put vile constructions on sufficiently innocent phrases in the play, and then to applaud them in a Satyr-like manner. Behind Mr. Goodchild, with a party of other Lunatics and one Keeper, the express incarnation of the thing called a 'gent.' A gentleman born; a gent manufactured. A something with a scarf round its neck, and a slipshod speech issuing from behind the scarf; more depraved, more foolish, more ignorant, more unable to believe in any noble or good thing of any kind, than the stupidest Bosjesman. The thing is but a boy in years, and is addled with drink. To do its company justice, even its company is ashamed of it, as it drawls its slang criticisms on the representation, and inflames Mr. Goodchild with a burning ardour to fling it into the pit. Its remarks are so horrible, that Mr. Goodchild, for the moment, even doubts whether that IS a wholesome Art, which sets women apart on a high floor before such a thing as this, though as good as its own sisters, or its own mother – whom Heaven forgive for bringing it into the world! But, the consideration that a low nature must make a low world of its own to live in, whatever the real materials, or it could no more exist than any of us could without the sense of touch, brings Mr. Goodchild to reason: the rather, because the thing soon drops its downy chin upon its scarf, and slobbers itself asleep.

Friday Morning. Early fights. Gong-donkey, and correct cards. Again, a great set towards the races, though not so great a set as on Wednesday. Much packing going on too, upstairs at the gunsmith's, the wax-chandler's, and the serious stationer's; for there will be a heavy drift of Lunatics and Keepers to London by the afternoon train. The course as pretty as ever; the great pincushion as like a pincushion, but not nearly so full of pins; whole rows of pins wanting. On the great event of the day, both Lunatics and Keepers become inspired with rage; and there is a violent scuffling, and a rushing at the losing jockey, and an emergence of the said jockey from a swaying and menacing crowd, protected by friends, and looking the worse for wear; which is a rough proceeding, though animating to see from a pleasant distance. After the great event, rills begin to flow from the pincushion towards the railroad; the rills swell into rivers; the rivers soon unite into a lake. The lake floats Mr. Goodchild into Doncaster, past the Itinerant personage in black, by the wayside telling him from the vantage ground of a legibly printed placard on a pole that for all these things the Lord will bring him to judgment. No turtle and venison ordinary this evening; that is all over. No Betting at the rooms; nothing there but the plants in pots, which have, all the week, been stood about the entry to give it an innocent appearance, and which have sorely sickened by this time.

Saturday. Mr. Idle wishes to know at breakfast, what were those dreadful groanings in his bedroom doorway in the night? Mr. Goodchild answers, Nightmare. Mr. Idle repels the calumny, and calls the waiter. The Angel is very sorry – had intended to explain; but you see, gentlemen, there was a gentleman dined downstairs with two more, and he had lost a deal of money, and he would drink a deal of wine, and in the night he 'took the horrors,' and got up; and as his friends could do nothing with him he laid himself down and groaned at Mr. Idle's door. 'And he DID groan there,' Mr. Idle says; 'and you will please to imagine me inside, "taking the horrors" too!'

So far, the picture of Doncaster on the occasion of its great sporting anniversary, offers probably a general representation of the social condition of the town, in the past as well as in the present time. The sole local phenomenon of the current year, which may be considered as entirely unprecedented in its way, and which certainly claims, on that account, some slight share of notice, consists in the actual existence of one remarkable individual, who is sojourning in Doncaster, and who, neither directly nor indirectly, has anything at all to do, in any capacity whatever, with the racing amusements of the week. Ranging throughout the entire crowd that fills the town, and including the inhabitants as well as the visitors, nobody is to be found altogether disconnected with the business of the day, excepting this one unparalleled man. He does not bet on the races, like the sporting men. He does not assist the races, like the jockeys, starters, judges, and grooms. He does not look on at the races, like Mr. Goodchild and his fellow-spectators. He does not profit by the races, like the hotelkeepers and the tradespeople. He does not minister to the necessities of the races, like the booth-keepers, the postilions, the waiters, and the hawkers of Lists. He does not assist the attractions of the races, like the actors at the theatre, the riders at the circus, or the posturers at the Poses Plastiques. Absolutely and literally, he is the only individual in Doncaster who stands by the brink of the full-flowing race-stream, and is not swept away by it in common with all the rest of his species. Who is this modern hermit, this recluse of the St. Leger-week, this inscrutably ungregarious being, who lives apart from the amusements and activities of his fellow-creatures? Surely, there is little difficulty in guessing that clearest and easiest of all riddles. Who could he be, but Mr. Thomas Idle?

Thomas had suffered himself to be taken to Doncaster, just as he would have suffered himself to be taken to any other place in the habitable globe which would guarantee him the temporary possession of a comfortable sofa to rest his ankle on. Once established at the hotel, with his leg on one cushion and his back against another, he formally declined taking the slightest interest in any circumstance whatever connected with the races, or with the people who were assembled to see them. Francis Goodchild, anxious that the hours should pass by his crippled travelling-companion as lightly as possible, suggested that his sofa should be moved to the window, and that he should amuse himself by looking out at the moving panorama of humanity, which the view from it of the principal street presented. Thomas, however, steadily declined profiting by the suggestion.

'The farther I am from the window,' he said, 'the better, Brother Francis, I shall be pleased. I have nothing in common with the one prevalent idea of all those people who are passing in the street. Why should I care to look at them?'

'I hope I have nothing in common with the prevalent idea of a great many of them, either,' answered Goodchild, thinking of the sporting gentlemen whom he had met in the course of his wanderings about Doncaster. 'But, surely, among all the people who are walking by the house, at this very moment, you may find–'

'Not one living creature,' interposed Thomas, 'who is not, in one way or another, interested in horses, and who is not, in a greater or less degree, an admirer of them. Now, I hold opinions in reference to these particular members of the quadruped creation, which may lay claim (as I believe) to the disastrous distinction of being unpartaken by any other human being, civilised or savage, over the whole surface of the earth. Taking the horse as an animal in the abstract, Francis, I cordially despise him from every point of view.'

'Thomas,' said Goodchild, 'confinement to the house has begun to affect your biliary secretions. I shall go to the chemist's and get you some physic.'

'I object,' continued Thomas, quietly possessing himself of his friend's hat, which stood on a table near him,–'I object, first, to the personal appearance of the horse. I protest against the conventional idea of beauty, as attached to that animal. I think his nose too long, his forehead too low, and his legs (except in the case of the carthorse) ridiculously thin by comparison with the size of his body. Again, considering how big an animal he is, I object to the contemptible delicacy of his constitution. Is he not the sickliest creature in creation? Does any child catch cold as easily as a horse? Does he not sprain his fetlock, for all his appearance of superior strength, as easily as I sprained my ankle! Furthermore, to take him from another point of view, what a helpless wretch he is! No fine lady requires more constant waiting-on than a horse. Other animals can make their own toilette: he must have a groom. You will tell me that this is because we want to make his coat artificially glossy. Glossy! Come home with me, and see my cat, – my clever cat, who can groom herself! Look at your own dog! see how the intelligent creature currycombs himself with his own honest teeth! Then, again, what a fool the horse is, what a poor, nervous fool! He will start at a piece of white paper in the road as if it was a lion. His one idea, when he hears a noise that he is not accustomed to, is to run away from it. What do you say to those two common instances of the sense and courage of this absurdly overpraised animal? I might multiply them to two hundred, if I chose to exert my mind and waste my breath, which I never do. I prefer coming at once to my last charge against the horse, which is the most serious of all, because it affects his moral character. I accuse him boldly, in his capacity of servant to man, of slyness and treachery. I brand him publicly, no matter how mild he may look about the eyes, or how sleek he may be about the coat, as a systematic betrayer, whenever he can get the chance, of the confidence reposed in him. What do you mean by laughing and shaking your head at me?'

'Oh, Thomas, Thomas!' said Goodchild. 'You had better give me my hat; you had better let me get you that physic.'

'I will let you get anything you like, including a composing draught for yourself,' said Thomas, irritably alluding to his fellow-apprentice's inexhaustible activity, 'if you will only sit quiet for five minutes longer, and hear me out. I say again the horse is a betrayer of the confidence reposed in him; and that opinion, let me add, is drawn from my own personal experience, and is not based on any fanciful theory whatever. You shall have two instances, two overwhelming instances. Let me start the first of these by asking, what is the distinguishing quality which the Shetland Pony has arrogated to himself, and is still perpetually trumpeting through the world by means of popular report and books on Natural History? I see the answer in your face: it is the quality of being sure-footed. He professes to have other virtues, such as hardiness and strength, which you may discover on trial; but the one thing which he insists on your believing, when you get on his back, is that he may be safely depended on not to tumble down with you. Very good. Some years ago, I was in Shetland with a party of friends. They insisted on taking me with them to the top of a precipice that overhung the sea. It was a great distance off, but they all determined to walk to it except me. I was wiser then than I was with you at Carrock, and I determined to be carried to the precipice. There was no carriage-road in the island, and nobody offered (in consequence, as I suppose, of the imperfectly-civilised state of the country) to bring me a sedan-chair, which is naturally what I should have liked best. A Shetland pony was produced instead. I remembered my Natural History, I recalled popular report, and I got on the little beast's back, as any other man would have done in my position, placing implicit confidence in the sureness of his feet. And how did he repay that confidence? Brother Francis, carry your mind on from morning to noon. Picture to yourself a howling wilderness of grass and bog, bounded by low stony hills. Pick out one particular spot in that imaginary scene, and sketch me in it, with outstretched arms, curved back, and heels in the air, plunging headforemost into a black patch of water and mud. Place just behind me the legs, the body, and the head of a sure-footed Shetland pony, all stretched flat on the ground, and you will have produced an accurate representation of a very lamentable fact. And the moral device, Francis, of this picture will be to testify that when gentlemen put confidence in the legs of Shetland ponies, they will find to their cost that they are leaning on nothing but broken reeds. There is my first instance – and what have you got to say to that?'

'Nothing, but that I want my hat,' answered Goodchild, starting up and walking restlessly about the room.

'You shall have it in a minute,' rejoined Thomas. 'My second instance' – (Goodchild groaned, and sat down again) – 'My second instance is more appropriate to the present time and place, for it refers to a racehorse. Two years ago an excellent friend of mine, who was desirous of prevailing on me to take regular exercise, and who was well enough acquainted with the weakness of my legs to expect no very active compliance with his wishes on their part, offered to make me a present of one of his horses. Hearing that the animal in question had started in life on the turf, I declined accepting the gift with many thanks; adding, by way of explanation, that I looked on a racehorse as a kind of embodied hurricane, upon which no sane man of my character and habits could be expected to seat himself. My friend replied that, however appropriate my metaphor might be as applied to racehorses in general, it was singularly unsuitable as applied to the particular horse which he proposed to give me. From a foal upwards this remarkable animal had been the idlest and most sluggish of his race. Whatever capacities for speed he might possess he had kept so strictly to himself, that no amount of training had ever brought them out. He had been found hopelessly slow as a racer, and hopelessly lazy as a hunter, and was fit for nothing but a quiet, easy life of it with an old gentleman or an invalid. When I heard this account of the horse, I don't mind confessing that my heart warmed to him. Visions of Thomas Idle ambling serenely on the back of a steed as lazy as himself, presenting to a restless world the soothing and composite spectacle of a kind of sluggardly Centaur, too peaceable in his habits to alarm anybody, swam attractively before my eyes. I went to look at the horse in the stable. Nice fellow! he was fast asleep with a kitten on his back. I saw him taken out for an airing by the groom. If he had had trousers on his legs I should not have known them from my own, so deliberately were they lifted up, so gently were they put down, so slowly did they get over the ground. From that moment I gratefully accepted my friend's offer. I went home; the horse followed me – by a slow train. Oh, Francis, how devoutly I believed in that horse I how carefully I looked after all his little comforts! I had never gone the length of hiring a manservant to wait on myself; but I went to the expense of hiring one to wait upon him. If I thought a little of myself when I bought the softest saddle that could be had for money, I thought also of my horse. When the man at the shop afterwards offered me spurs and a whip, I turned from him with horror. When I sallied out for my first ride, I went purposely unarmed with the means of hurrying my steed. He proceeded at his own pace every step of the way; and when he stopped, at last, and blew out both his sides with a heavy sigh, and turned his sleepy head and looked behind him, I took him home again, as I might take home an artless child who said to me, "If you please, sir, I am tired." For a week this complete harmony between me and my horse lasted undisturbed. At the end of that time, when he had made quite sure of my friendly confidence in his laziness, when he had thoroughly acquainted himself with all the little weaknesses of my seat (and their name is Legion), the smouldering treachery and ingratitude of the equine nature blazed out in an instant. Without the slightest provocation from me, with nothing passing him at the time but a pony-chaise driven by an old lady, he started in one instant from a state of sluggish depression to a state of frantic high spirits. He kicked, he plunged, he shied, he pranced, he capered fearfully. I sat on him as long as I could, and when I could sit no longer, I fell off. No, Francis! this is not a circumstance to be laughed at, but to be wept over. What would be said of a Man who had requited my kindness in that way? Range over all the rest of the animal creation, and where will you find me an instance of treachery so black as this? The cow that kicks down the milking-pail may have some reason for it; she may think herself taxed too heavily to contribute to the dilution of human tea and the greasing of human bread. The tiger who springs out on me unawares has the excuse of being hungry at the time, to say nothing of the further justification of being a total stranger to me. The very flea who surprises me in my sleep may defend his act of assassination on the ground that I, in my turn, am always ready to murder him when I am awake. I defy the whole body of Natural Historians to move me, logically, off the ground that I have taken in regard to the horse. Receive back your hat, Brother Francis, and go to the chemist's, if you please; for I have now done. Ask me to take anything you like, except an interest in the Doncaster races. Ask me to look at anything you like, except an assemblage of people all animated by feelings of a friendly and admiring nature towards the horse. You are a remarkably well-informed man, and you have heard of hermits. Look upon me as a member of that ancient fraternity, and you will sensibly add to the many obligations which Thomas Idle is proud to owe to Francis Goodchild.'

Here, fatigued by the effort of excessive talking, disputatious Thomas waved one hand languidly, laid his head back on the sofa-pillow, and calmly closed his eyes.

At a later period, Mr. Goodchild assailed his travelling companion boldly from the impregnable fortress of common sense. But Thomas, though tamed in body by drastic discipline, was still as mentally unapproachable as ever on the subject of his favourite delusion.

The view from the window after Saturday's breakfast is altogether changed. The tradesmen's families have all come back again. The serious stationer's young woman of all work is shaking a duster out of the window of the combination breakfast-room; a child is playing with a doll, where Mr. Thurtell's hair was brushed; a sanitary scrubbing is in progress on the spot where Mr. Palmer's braces were put on. No signs of the Races are in the streets, but the tramps and the tumbledown-carts and trucks laden with drinking-forms and tables and remnants of booths, that are making their way out of the town as fast as they can. The Angel, which has been cleared for action all the week, already begins restoring every neat and comfortable article of furniture to its own neat and comfortable place. The Angel's daughters (pleasanter angels Mr. Idle and Mr. Goodchild never saw, nor more quietly expert in their business, nor more superior to the common vice of being above it), have a little time to rest, and to air their cheerful faces among the flowers in the yard. It is market-day. The market looks unusually natural, comfortable, and wholesome; the market-people too. The town seems quite restored, when, hark! a metallic bray – The Gong-donkey!

The wretched animal has not cleared off with the rest, but is here, under the window. How much more inconceivably drunk now, how much more begrimed of paw, how much more tight of calico hide, how much more stained and daubed and dirty and dunghilly, from his horrible broom to his tender toes, who shall say! He cannot even shake the bray out of himself now, without laying his cheek so near to the mud of the street, that he pitches over after delivering it. Now, prone in the mud, and now backing himself up against shop-windows, the owners of which come out in terror to remove him; now, in the drinking-shop, and now in the tobacconist's, where he goes to buy tobacco, and makes his way into the parlour, and where he gets a cigar, which in half-a-minute he forgets to smoke; now dancing, now dozing, now cursing, and now complimenting My Lord, the Colonel, the Noble Captain, and Your Honourable Worship, the Gong-donkey kicks up his heels, occasionally braying, until suddenly, he beholds the dearest friend he has in the world coming down the street.

The dearest friend the Gong-donkey has in the world, is a sort of Jackall, in a dull, mangy, black hide, of such small pieces that it looks as if it were made of blacking bottles turned inside out and cobbled together. The dearest friend in the world (inconceivably drunk too) advances at the Gong-donkey, with a hand on each thigh, in a series of humorous springs and stops, wagging his head as he comes. The Gong-donkey regarding him with attention and with the warmest affection, suddenly perceives that he is the greatest enemy he has in the world, and hits him hard in the countenance. The astonished Jackall closes with the Donkey, and they roll over and over in the mud, pummelling one another. A Police Inspector, supernaturally endowed with patience, who has long been looking on from the Guildhall-steps, says, to a myrmidon, 'Lock 'em up! Bring 'em in!'

Appropriate finish to the Grand Race-Week. The Gong-donkey, captive and last trace of it, conveyed into limbo, where they cannot do better than keep him until next Race-Week. The Jackall is wanted too, and is much looked for, over the way and up and down. But, having had the good fortune to be undermost at the time of the capture, he has vanished into air.

On Saturday afternoon, Mr. Goodchild walks out and looks at the Course. It is quite deserted; heaps of broken crockery and bottles are raised to its memory; and correct cards and other fragments of paper are blowing about it, as the regulation little paper-books, carried by the French soldiers in their breasts, were seen, soon after the battle was fought, blowing idly about the plains of Waterloo.

Where will these present idle leaves be blown by the idle winds, and where will the last of them be one day lost and forgotten? An idle question, and an idle thought; and with it Mr. Idle fitly makes his bow, and Mr. Goodchild his, and thus ends the Lazy Tour of Two Idle Apprentices.

www.ReadHowYouWant.com

You can buy our **Large Type** and **EasyRead** books from our www.ReadHowYouWant.com website, from websites like Amazon.com and through your UK and North American bookshop.

EasyRead books are designed to make your reading easy and enjoyable. **EasyRead** books are published in different font sizes, so you can select the font size best for you.

EasyRead is for people with normal eyesight who want books in an easy-to-read format.

EasyRead Comfort is for people who find reading small print tiring but do not need large print.

EasyRead Large is for people who find it easier to read larger print.

The **EasyRead** font, character, word and line spacing have all been set to make it as easy as possible both to recognize a word, and to run your eye along a line of text without losing your place. We split as few words as possible at line ends, as split words make reading harder and can be annoying. For out-of-copyright books, words have been changed to modern spelling (where the sense is not affected), and the original hyphenation of compound words has been retained where this improves word recognition or sense.

With most things you buy, you get a choice, and you can choose the make and model that suits best. There is a big exception – books. You don't get to choose a format that is easy for you to read – you have to read the format the publisher selects.

This "One Size Fits All" paradigm no longer need apply to books.

At www.ReadHowYouWant.com, you can order a book just as you want it, so you can read it easily. You can choose nearly any format, and at a surprisingly low cost, because of a technical breakthrough that allows us to typeset an individual book automatically, print and bind the book and have it quickly sent directly to you.

You can have your book in **Talking Book** formats (**DAISY or MP3**) or as an **E-book** or in **Braille**.

We have developed totally new visual formats which we hope will help people with **dyslexia** and other print reading disabilities. Look at www.ReadHowYo uWant.com for more information.

Good news for publishers and authors. There is a big market for large type, personalized and accessible format books. We can help publishers and authors find new market opportunities for their books, and selling your book through www.ReadH owYouWant.com is easy – we do the work for you. Contact us on info@ReadHowYouWant.com.